I0620832

Pleasure as a Higher Calling

No Regrets

Spicy Stories of Life, Love, Sensuality, and Lust

SAVANNAH ARIES

Pleasure Press

The events depicted in these stories are fictitious.
Any similarity to any person living or dead is coincidental.
The stories are merely a lush figment of the author's vivid imagination.

Dedicated to lovers . . .
all of you.

Books by Savannah Aries in the
Pleasure as a Higher Calling series:

Waking Up

Easy & Delicious

No Regrets

Contents

Foreword

What Savannah Says About
Pleasure as a State of Mind

Do you often find yourself adrift in pleasurable daydreams and imagined flights of fancy? Are you prone to rearranging difficult situations in your mind to better suit your own sense of reality?

I understand that. Some of us tend to take it to the limit.

When society's collective consciousness puts pressure on us for deviating from the agreed-upon norm, we who prefer to set our own limits feel obligated to peel off that indoctrination like a 1950s pointy bra and girdle—like a scratchy old sweater—like a familiar doctrine that inherently destroys our joy, our good life, our *joie d'vivre*.

One day I woke up and realized that Pleasure could be my Higher Calling.

It sounded indulgent, even a bit obscene. Those were my first thoughts and honestly, I immediately set to dissuading myself, having been accused more than once of living in denial and not taking seriously the harsh version of reality on the nightly news. Like anyone else, I am completely aware of those horror shows. They hurt my heart and my hope. My decision to adjust my reality to include daily doses of fun, laughter and pleasure didn't alter the fearful and wretched news, but it did alter the kinds of stories I focused my attention on.

There are good, heartwarming, optimistic stories and solutions happening every day around the world if you care to look for them.

So if you were to tell me you also long for a little more pleasure in your life, I'd share what I've learned: Pleasure is a state of mind. If you were to say you love to dance, sing, laugh, walk by the sea or in the forest, prepare and enjoy delicious food, make love with a *simpatico* partner, then I get it about you. And if you were to confide that yes, although in theory you'd love to adopt pleasure as a state of mind, you realize that you've been conditioned to believe such thinking indecent or disgusting. Well, I also understand that ancient lie. Perhaps you'll allow me to help you recognize how seeking pleasure can alleviate despair, bring you a sense of well-being, or even enhance your immune system.

When I decided to look for the pleasure in all I think and do, I boosted my immunity against the polarized talking heads shouting on my TV. I realized that I could stay well informed and more resilient if I didn't indulge in sensational negativity, however it presented itself. When I notice the vacant eyes of people leaning on their carts in the market or feel the tension of those rushing madly through their day or witness moms flicking through their phones at the playground—scarcely able to glance away when their child calls out "Mommy, look . . . watch me!"—I'm reminded again and again why the concept of Pleasure as a Higher Calling is right for me and my personal well-being.

I trust that all pleasure is a gift from the Divine. All sensual delight is offered to us for free. All the things we inherently love to do have pleasure associated with them. We can elevate our awareness of bringing pleasure into our lives if we want to. Our imaginations are worth cultivating because pleasure is a state of mind, not of circumstance.

There's another reason I bring this up. In my view, the most interesting activity in the universe is creative and sensual at its core. Have you watched footage from the Hubble space telescope when two galaxies collide in a spectacular mating dance of extravagant light and color? Or sat in a garden and watched the birds and bees flit from flower to flower on a sensual mission of pollination? What about delighting in preparing your favorite meal, savoring the colors, textures, aromas, and flavors that elicit the pleasure of eating that follows? Or how about when you've listened to rapturous music or read a significant poem or stood before an artist's creation and allowed your senses to indulge and transport you? All these and more are pleasures to me, and no doubt you could elaborate upon them. They may not be the same deliciousness experienced when making love with the one whose body and soul intimately touch and move you, but pleasure is important for its own sake and can be found anywhere.

When I realized that my state of mind determines my perception and awareness, I began to train myself to seek pleasure in the mundane as well as the sublime. It feels so good to complete a tedious task or overcome a difficult challenge when I explore, cultivate, practice, and reward the principle of pleasure as a consciousness in my daily life.

Some time ago a wise older friend asked me; "Savannah dear, how would you prefer to live your life?" We had been sharing some of our difficult experiences and I caught myself wondering why the troubled painful memories stuck like barbed wire while the many wonderful moments of happiness and pleasure drifted out of my embrace.

It was then that the mindset of Pleasure as a Higher Calling planted itself as my *raison d'être* and in time afforded me the daily joy I knew I deserved. What's true is that we all deserve love, joy, and pleasure. What is also true is that often we must make a decision to forage for pleasure in our daily life. We have little to lose and much to gain by setting an intention to find the pleasure in this life. It may take a bit of practice, maybe a 21-day-habit challenge, but whatever it takes, a fuller, richer, more nourishing point of view is worth it.

The Spicy Stories

We do not know what is on the other side of the storm.
~ Brian Francis

Fishing In Rio

My mother loved that '60s bossa nova song, "The Girl from Ipanema." I can still hear it: "Tall and tan and young and lovely . . ." Could she have pictured me, strolling along this expanse of white sand in Rio de Janeiro? That's hard to imagine. She never adjusted to—nor did she approve of—her daughters in bikinis. And even as a devoted sun worshiper, she would never have considered traveling this far from home.

I'm certainly neither tall nor tan, this being early November, after a stunningly short Pacific Northwest summer, and only my second week in the southern hemisphere. *Young?* Well, certainly still of heart and mind, but chronologically? Not exactly. And what about *lovely?* Some would still say so, bless them. But I am definitely *not* the girl from Ipanema. I am, instead, a mature contemporary woman who unabashedly enjoys wearing a skimpy bikini and intends to do so until I can no longer walk along the water's edge.

Are heads turning? Yes, but this is what I know for sure: It is not because I look fabulous in this tiny bit of cloth. I do not belong on the cover of a *Sports Illustrated* swimsuit edition and never have. Nor is it because I am fair-skinned and blonde, an unusual sight on this beach in off-season Rio. Walking along this stretch lined with resort hotels, I can't help but notice that under most of the side-by-side yellow umbrellas lie listless aging tourists very likely looking to beat Carnival and season prices. In comparison, I could feel smug, but what would be the point?

I've been told that what turns heads toward me is the recognition of a subtly attractive air of timeless sensuality. I believe that it is because I exude a certain confidence that accompanies me at this time of life and which can be sensed by both men and women as I pass by. That I am not tall and tan and young doesn't seem to register. Not with them, nor with me. *That,* I consider lovely.

And the joy I am experiencing this morning, walking the beach in Ipanema again after so long away, must be visible. I stroll with the hint of sway, a feeling of *Samba.* The softness of the sand provokes a lilt in my movements. One man I've passed each day thus far announces to me that I walk with a swagger but what I feel is the rhythm of music in my step. I can wander for miles along these beaches and feel like I'm dancing. What a blessing to be barefoot in the sand, soaking up the sun. Does it matter now that my skin is freckled and sun ruined from years of these pleasures? Each random dip into the ocean as I meander, caresses me, heals me, encourages me and the only thing I have to say is . . . Aaahh!

Along a less populated area of beach, I pass a man who waves enthusiastically to me. I nod without recognition but he stops and attempts to engage me in conversation. I don't speak much Portuguese. I think he is asking me if I have been swimming. I reply, "*Claro.*" Of course.

He reaches for my hand, which I do not offer in return. He is persistent and effusive and seems not to notice my lack of receptivity. "*Voce Inglesia.*" You are English. I stare at him without answering. "*Inglesia,*" he repeats and touches my thigh.

I point at him and say firmly, "*Nao me toque.*" Don't touch me.

But he touches me again, this time placing his hand on the small of my back. "*Você é muito linda, Inglesia. Venha comigo.*" You are very lovely, English. Come with me.

His face receives the quick thrust of my open palm. "*Pará-lo! Nao me toque novemente!*" Stop it! Don't touch me again! He backs away from me now, smiling, bowing, thrusting his hands in the air as if I had commanded him to reach for the sky. Once he is sufficiently behind me, I try to put him out of my mind and continue on my way.

But now another man approaches me. He has seen this encounter and asks if I need help. Did it look that way? I hadn't thought so, but say it's kind of him to ask. This one speaks English, although with an accent I can't distinguish. He tells me he takes me for an American.

I ask, "Couldn't it be possible that I am Canadian?"

He answers firmly, "No, you are American." He explains, "American take no shit from nobody; it's how you walk. American walk like owning the land in front of each step you taking." I laugh and tell him I'm actually Irish. He says, "No, you are certainly American." I suggest that I could be Swedish. Then he laughs too and says, "Only sassy American still be talking with me at this point." I'm left to ponder what this means. As I pass him, he calls back to me, "You are lovely, aging well. Definitely American." And there it is again: the phenomenon of aging brought to the fore, yes, hopefully aging well, but somehow the fact is always noticed.

I once read that when asked about aging with grace, Sophia Loren said something to the effect that a woman must always stand tall. Is she referring to posture or posturing? She also said that a beautiful woman must never sigh as if tired and surely never moan as if her body ached. And even if so, she must definitely not walk as though this were true. Also, I believe she said, no farting out loud, ever.

Her advice is sound, and since she's a pro at aging beautifully I will heed her words. I might add that in my experience, allowing oneself to be vulnerable and open to new adventures can be captivating. Exuding an aura of approachability and welcome is also important. But at the same time, being able to establish an authoritative boundary and mean it is useful as well. For example: holding one's ground to reproach undesired attention from, say, an aggressive sun-grizzled man on the beach. After all, it's not that I think I'm invincible but along with being a reasonably capable woman, I *am* an American and *I don't take no shit from nobody*, as he discovered quickly enough.

Further down the shore toward the neighborhoods of the Leblon, where I am staying, I see a young man casting his line, fishing from the beach. I've come upon him here at this time most mornings as I walk. I'm curious about what he expects to catch and try to ask him if he's been lucky today.

"Yes, I am lucky, Madame, but not so far today," he says in rapid Portuguese.

"*O que você vai pegar?*" What will you catch? is what I hope I am asking him.

"*O que eu puder!*" He laughs, and hands me his line to hold for good luck. I have no idea what *eu puder* means, but I'm pretty sure he said something about good luck.

"*Com prazer.*" With pleasure! One of the few phrases I know for sure.

I like the way his wooden spool, carved with mermaids, feels in my hand. I lay the line over my index finger just like I used to when I fished as a kid before I acquired fancy rods and reels. It's impossible not to notice that he is beautiful—almost innocent, seemingly unconcerned with time or even the catch. Perhaps he is fishing just for the pure pleasure of it.

I've always loved to fish as well and holding his line reminds me of the many hours of contentment I have experienced casting about wondering what might nibble on my bait. This bawdy thought and its juicy *double entendre* provokes me to a grin and I am unable to resist the laughter that bubbles up from my belly. He looks at me with a quizzical smile but makes no comment. I am lucky to have come upon him again this morning. Just standing together in the surf in hopeful anticipation of a catch—without the difficulty of conversation in two languages—is a pleasure in itself.

I'd like to know his name though, and ask, "*Qual é o seu nome de meu amigo?*" What is your name, my friend?

"*Feliciano. E qual é o seu nome senhora feliz?*" And what is your name happy lady?

"*Meu nome é Savannah.*" Yes, I am happy, like the meaning of his name.

He looks at me with intense but smiling eyes and nods. I am astounded at my sudden ability to understand and carry on even a simple conversation in Portuguese. It may be textbook, like Google Translator, but at least I feel that we are somehow communicating. A strange sense of contentedness overcomes me standing next to him.

Feliciano points to the line in my hand at the same moment I feel the tug. I instinctively yank it hard to set the hook but then hand it back to its owner. While he quickly and expertly winds his line around the carved wooden stick, I step back and watch him wrestle with the catch on the other end. It's a good one, frisky and leaping out of the sea in an attempt to be free of us.

The muscles on this beautiful young man's back and shoulders ripple as he digs his feet into the sand, bracing himself against the waves pushing then pulling at his strong calves. For a brief moment my eyes are transfixed on his body. He is about six feet tall, bronzed from head to toe, with dark curls over his ears, and he is young. How much younger is hard to say because he is so open and friendly and seems quite at ease with me. I register a familiar flutter in my tummy and the pleasure of a tingle just below that.

But now he is landing his prize. It's a decent catch, I think he is trying to tell me, about three or four kilos of Yellowfin. He is obviously pleased, his broad smile and gleaming white teeth a confirmation.

"*Ver? Sorte hoje por causa de você Senhora Savannah.*" See? Lucky today because of you Ms. Savannah.

I am lucky to meet you today, is what I am feeling but who knows how to say that? "*Eu sou feliz.*" I am happy, is what I can come up with.

He unsheathes a knife and starts to clean the fish. What should I say now? I'd like to fish again with beautiful Feliciano, but all I can muster is, "*Vê lo novamente um dia em breve, espero.*" See you again one day soon I hope.

"Yes, I hope too, Senhora Savannah." What? He speaks English after all? I have to laugh. As I have mentioned, my Portuguese is very weak, although I guess he understood me well enough.

"Maybe tomorrow?" I ask. Can he imagine the possibilities tomorrow may bring? I am beginning to glimpse several.

"Maybe." He smiles, then waves to me as I watch him walk briskly down the beach, his cleaned fish hung and swinging from his line. What a delightful encounter.

But for the rest of this day I have nothing more pressing to attend to than my own wistfulness. I'm ready to go back to my lovely *casa pequeña* now, to enjoy some fruit and coffee on the terrace while I muse on life and how best to live it. The pursuit of pleasure is never far from my musings. Writing about it is what I plan to do today.

Tonight, however, I will dine alone. I've already noted that there are few single men here and those that might be found along that strip of hotels further toward Ipanema, either are—or act as if they are—ancient. I can easily overlook a balding head and wrinkles, even the inevitable lack of vitality. But when I see one walking as if every cell in his body hurts to do it, with teeth stained from cigars and neglect, man boobs, or desperately sucking in a tummy bucket? I'm sorry. No.

Even so, if these men are still breathing without an oxygen tank or not legally blind then they are certainly gaping at the many beautiful young women who inhabit this place and no doubt engaging in fantasies that involve a miracle. My libido follows my eye so how can I be critical of a pastime with so much imaginative pleasure in it?

There are charming men here too, of course, and if they are of a certain age or stature and not gay then they are married or have a young beauty on their arm. And what about the plentiful eye candy? Well, these are mostly vendors, waiters, or hustlers and of no interest to me. But now a young fisherman by the name of Feliciano is beginning to figure into my musings on pleasure. I will be searching for more than unusual shells as I walk tomorrow.

As it happens, when I return to my new home, I find myself busied with rearranging the furnishings, puttering in the small terrace garden, washing the windows, the floor, and my clothing, doing anything but sitting down to write. I glance occasionally at my laptop sitting purposefully on the small table in the corner, where the shutters open to a view of brilliant, lush greens and flowers in shades of pink and orange within walls of my terrace. Standing in the center of this tiny but charming room with its faded peach stucco walls, I feel a familiar pang of neglect. It takes a concerted effort to ignore the fact that I am already failing to attend to my primary reason for being here.

Somehow the entire day passes with errands that find me wandering the busy market, discovering hidden shops and cafés, or peering through iron gates into courtyard gardens in the more posh estates of the Leblon. Standing on a corner now, I've lost my bearings and request directions from two women strolling with their babies. I've encountered them passing on my lane several times. I ask if we are neighbors. I really need to practice the language. My questions and comments bring giggles they can't conceal with polite, gentle corrections. Even their beautiful smiling babies think I am amusing. I'm glad we can laugh. I'd like to become friends.

I turn to go home, and see a small shop with lengths of fabric fluttering in the breeze. The fabrics are dyed in the most vivid colors and designs. The woman inside is sewing. Smiling, she waves me over and gestures to her samples. *"Bonita, sim?"* Beautiful, yes? She shows me a picture in a fashion magazine of a simple dress, cut on the bias to drape the body elegantly.

"Perfeito for you, *Senhora.* You *gosta* . . . you like this?

"I love it!" I nod affirmatively, my mind numb from earlier translation fatigue. She stands, pulling the tape from around her slim neck, and takes a few quick measurements. Choosing just one of her richly colored hand-dyed fabrics is impossible. I settle on three and I think she is indicating to me that she can design a dress using all of them.

"*Amanhã, Senhora.*" Tomorrow. "Very beautiful for you."

"*Obrigado, Senhora.*" I think it's *obrigado* or is it *gracias*? Knowing a little Spanish and less Portuguese, I am perpetually confused. It isn't until I open the gate to my terrace that I realize I didn't ask the price or any question at all. I only hope that I have managed to make the correct assumptions about our transaction. I may have just ordered three dresses but I'm too mentally exhausted to go back and try to communicate.

It's dusk and all I really want at the moment is a glass of chilled white wine and the will to write. Manifesting the glass of wine is easy. Mustering the will to write eludes me. Apparently my muse has abandoned me for the evening. I warm the remnants of yesterday's lunch, a spicy stuffed pepper, and sit quietly at the tiny table on my terrace until darkness falls around me and the insects discover my presence. My bed whispers to me, *come in, come in.*

I slowly awaken from a dream. It's a complex scenario with tangled lines of fish and a solemn parade of wheezing oxygen tanks. I am standing at the oven, naked but for a brilliantly colored flour-dusted apron cut on the bias draping only the essential minimum of my body. I'm baking lemony *malasada dois* for Carnival. In this dream, Feliciano has brought me a splendid fish and I present him with hot buns. He licks his luscious lips and devours the sweet buns then reaches for mine. A certain part of my body awakens and responds with juicy tingling and I absently touch myself with the delectable thought of Feliciano's hands on me. A flashing glimpse of gasping oxygen tanks brutally interrupts my reverie and the impulse to pleasure evaporates. It hasn't been a bad dream but neither is it refreshing. It's dawn, much earlier than is usual for me to be so wide awake. Unable to rekindle my desire, I decide to walk.

The market isn't open yet so I head toward the beach, stopping at a café for a Brazilian espresso. I sit and watch nearby shopkeepers open their colorfully painted shutters and doors; fanciful splashes of blue and orange, yellow and pink contrast with the whitewashed walls. The coffee is good and strong, an enjoyable tasty jolt. Something feels different in the air this morning but what is it? The monkeys chattering more loudly than usual in the trees overhead seem to notice it as well. The ocean beckons me to finish my sip, escape this racket, and get my feet wet.

Isn't this about the place I met the young fisherman yesterday, or was it further toward Ipanema? The air is strangely still and even the water stretching out to the rocky outer islands is smooth. No one is strolling, no one is fishing, no one is here at all. Perhaps this is not the spot. I continue along, mildly disappointed. Why? What is it I am hoping for? It's a bit premature to be projecting a story onto Feliciano so why am I doing it? Is it that he is beautiful and friendly? Or is it the comfortable discovery that language and therefore conversation needn't be such an arduous chore?

I remind myself once again of the purpose of my transplantation to Brazil at this time. I am here to escape a dreary northern winter. And I am here to write. Yes, I am here intentionally to write. I have been commissioned to write a story with Rio as the backdrop. But already I am distracting myself with fantasies of romance—or minimally carnal lust—with a probable impossibility. Well, this is what I do. I can't help myself. It entertains and inspires me, often feeding my imagination so that I may create a delicious story. My preference, however, is to live the story fully first.

My neglected keyboard beckons me back to my little bungalow near the further edge of the Leblon. I was thrilled to find this private colonial carriage house, converted now to a small but charmingly livable *casa* a few streets in from the beach. It's on a quiet cobblestone lane—an alley really—lined with orange trees and near one of the smaller open markets. The mornings are particularly delightful with the inviting aroma of the bakeries and cafés on this block. It suits me well for my northwest winter's stay in Rio's summer. And I will finish my manuscript. I will.

But in spite of this determination, my mind wanders back to a yearning for companionship, stimulating conversation, and glorious lovemaking. I'll need that and of course, it must be with the right one. I've allowed my mind to drift toward young Feliciano but that does not mean the feeling is mutual. Still, I know myself well. I am confident that I can concoct a scenario, a story that compels him to at least consider this possibility. Or I will meet a suitable other. Soon would be best.

I have been typing now for hours. I can't stop. I don't want to interrupt this enthusiastic fire I've finally kindled. Earlier, when I went to the market for provisions, I found a Yellowfin, much smaller than Feliciano's but just right for dinner tonight. Because of translation difficulties it might be a mackerel but who cares really? Garlic and lemon, some chilies, and a bit of creamy risotto with a glass of crisp Torrontés from Argentina will be my meal. I already look forward to it but first to complete this chapter.

I need to stretch and bend, take a moment to rest my eyes on something other than this screen. Perhaps a sip or two of Torrontés while I think will give me the added inspiration to make this work even more luscious and enjoyable. There is a breeze picking up now. It refreshes me as I settle back down to create in front of the window opened upon my lovely terrace. This wind is in from Africa and suddenly that old Joni Mitchell song about Cary, his cane, her silver, and the mermaid café are like a fragrance for my mind. I loved that song about being transplanted far from home. This North African wind carries a message for me: Something is coming on the wind. I can feel it.

The sun is about to set. I'm compelled to close my laptop and walk to the beach right now and wish it well on its journey to the other side of the world. Many others seem to have the same sentiment on this strangely beautiful evening. On the horizon, a thick bank of clouds follows the warm wind inland. I love this quieter part of the beach that fronts the neighborhoods of the Leblon. Families, children, and grandparents, displaying their affection for one another, stroll along the walk, sit in the cafés or lean on the low sea wall. I wander to the water's edge and invite the waves to kiss my feet and lick my calves.

What a sight! The sunset is beyond spectacular. The colors of the sky are a palette of blended hues. Oranges, purples, reds, and yellows discover each other's edges and embrace. The sun drops behind Two Brothers Mountain to the southwest where I imagine it splashing into the southern Atlantic.

"*Senhora* Savannah." My name is called, but who knows me here? No one is near. I glance behind me and discover the beautiful fisherman standing there.

"Oh! Feliciano. *O que é uma doce surpresa.*" What a sweet surprise!

"Will you speak English with me, *Senhora?* I wish to practice."

Oh my God, what a relief to hear this! "Gladly, although I need to practice my Portuguese too. It is so strenuous to make myself understood." Or at least it was until I met him and it started to flow a bit more easily. Strange.

"Strenuous? What does this word mean to speaking?"

"Oh, I guess I mean that trying to make myself understood in Portuguese is very difficult, exhausting really. Shopping at the market, using all the wrong words, has made this quite obvious to me." Stepping closer, he laughs as though he understands me. His gravity draws me like a magnet. Our feet sink into the wet sand and touch, settling alongside one another. "Isn't this one of the most gorgeous skies you've ever seen?"

"*Sim Senhora.* I mean yes. It is *gorgeous.* I like this word. I may call you Savannah?"

"Please, yes." Oh my! Yes, yes, yes you may.

Feliciano's smile is radiant. He makes a magnificent silhouette against this backdrop of breathtaking beauty. I am caught speechless in the moment. He appears to be comfortable with the silence which is a blessed reprieve to me. I hadn't expected this opportunity to meet him and now the thought of manipulating a passing fantasy into a possibility seems adolescent and unfitting. We stand staring out to sea at the bruised aubergine horizon.

Dusk slips into place with just the sliver of a new moon rising up through the urgently passing clouds. The weather is changing, into what I have no idea. The onshore African wind has become much more than a stiff breeze. It billows the thin cotton skirt I'm wearing and blows my hair across my face. I turn to tell Feliciano that it's time for me to head home and find him staring at me. Brushing my hair away from my face, he tucks it behind my ear. His touch relays an unspoken message. It has meaning but I don't dare translate. I haven't been my usual forward self. Why is that? Somehow I instinctively feel content to follow his lead, should he actually care to lead me.

We make our way to the promenade, wind pushing hard at our backs now. I ask him if he's heard a weather report declaring a storm brewing.

"Yes, *Senhora*, a storm. What is brewing mean?"

I laugh. "Stirring up, cooking up, whipping up—brewing."

"Oh! *Sim, mulher encantadora.*" Yes, enchanting woman. "A storm is brewing." Feliciano grins. Taking my hands in his, he pulls me close. What does this mean? My heart skips a quick beat and my thoughts get caught in the wind. I am not really confused, but I am surprised. And I am again, uncharacteristically, at a loss for words.

Gazing into his mischievous dark eyes, searching for a clue to his thoughts, I wonder suddenly how it is that we are at the same beach at the same moment sharing the sunset, bracing ourselves against a coming storm? He has taken a stance against the wind, protecting me from its increasing force. My skirt is plastered like a second skin around my thighs.

Without warning a passing Vespa swerves into me with enough force to topple me over. The rider regains his balance and keeps going as I tumble to the ground. Feliciano curses loudly at him, his words swallowed by the wind. Kneeling to assist me he inspects the raw scrapes on my arm and thigh, now beginning to bleed.

"*Senhora, meu Deus!* Are you okay? *Filho da puta! Estúpido!* Fucking idiot! I take you home now. Where do we go?"

He gently helps me to stand. I am dizzy and unbalanced. The wind shoves me against him. His arms encircle me. He holds me touching my cheek tenderly before leaning down to pull the cloth of my skirt, an inadvertent bloody bandage, away from the scrape on my thigh to inspect it again.

"We go now, *Senhora. Que maneira?*" Which way?

The scrapes sting but don't hurt badly, so why do I feel as though I am about to cry? It must be the wind in my eyes inducing these tears. I am touched by his kindness, a strange combination of fierce gentleness and authority. I still can't find a single word and point toward where we need to go, toward my street, toward my new home. His concern is compelling and it stirs up lost emotions I haven't felt in many years of strident independence. I haven't leaned on anyone for such a long time. I feel as weak and vulnerable as a child. Why am I caught up in such a blustering tempest of feeling over a minor scrape?

"*Ferir?* Hurting? I mean, do you pain? What I mean? *Senhora* Savannah, you not speak? *Por quê?*" Why?

I don't know why. I am not myself. Who am I then? Am I not a wordsmith, an author, a storyteller, a mature contemporary woman of a certain age? Isn't this how I always describe myself? I've been knocked silly but it isn't due to an errant biker or even the wind. The glory of color and beauty splashed across this southern sky would only add to my usual loquaciousness. And it can't be because a *gorgeous* young man has his arm around me. That, of course, is wonderful, but not exactly a new experience.

The thoughts that flood my mind are about fishing in Rio. I wanted to. I hadn't thought much about how I would go about that or what I might catch, only the meditative pleasure of the activity. The metaphor playing out before me is fascinating. I exerted no volition beyond a passing playful musing and the Gods stirred up a storyline, created a storm, provided a mini-crisis and a gallant rescue, the ingredients for any compelling story. The next chapter is open, unwritten.

"*Senhora* Savannah, *por favor,* tell me *o que está errado*?" What is wrong? "*Por favor, Senhora.* Speak with me."

"Oh, *eu sinto muito.*" I'm so sorry. "I am OK. Don't worry, *por favor.*"

He seems unconvinced. Glancing around I notice we have already passed my lane by several blocks. What the hell? I am not hurt badly. I didn't hit my head so why have I become so, I don't know, weird and disoriented? We passed my street. Maybe that means I should continue on alone, thank him for his help, *not* invite him to my place. Now I know I've come undone. Not invite him into my home? When would I ever consider that a viable option? Never! Especially ridiculous now considering it is this beautiful man who is showing me such kindness and concern. *Estúpido!* Very stupid, indeed!

"We passed my street. My place is this way." He puts his arm around me and steers me in the right direction. I feel completely helpless. I need to sit down.

When we come to the gate, we discover that the wind has knocked over and shattered the wine glass I left on the ledge of the wall enclosing my courtyard terrace. I stare at it, fascinated, as if it were some rarity or great work of art. It's dark now and I search for the light switch. I realize I have no idea where it is since I'm still relatively unfamiliar with my little cottage. I only use the lamp I found at a flea market. Its beautiful silk shade is washed in tones of fuschia and I much prefer the light through its softer, more sensual hues.

But now, Feliciano is all business not waiting for direction from me, which is fortunate, since I've collapsed into a chair and am quite useless. He goes to the sink and fills a bowl with warm water and sea salt, finds a soft cloth and carefully begins to clean my wounds despite my moans and grimaces. Again, I feel a welling of tears but not from the sting. This emotion is more a remembrance of being lovingly tended to as a child. Embedded in these feelings emerges a deep longing for the truest and sweetest of lost connections. I begin to weep.

Alarmed, Feliciano stops for a moment and seems uncertain how to continue. I vaguely notice that without the use of words to express myself, feelings arise organically, unedited by thoughts about what they mean. I can't instruct him; I don't have the right words. We can't have the conversation that would take me out of my heart and back into my head.

In the past my occasional reluctant tears have caused men great discomfort, initiating a call for explanation, a need for the tears to stop, a need to fix the problem, a need to relieve their own anxiety, but rarely a willingness to understand or even simply allow this feminine mystery. I learned to stem the flow quickly and freeze the emotion, avoiding the disappointment of expecting more. I've learned I can will my tears to stop and I try to do that now. But his warmth and his care threaten to melt what's been frozen and forgotten for years into a tsunami of tears. The ends of the silk scarf around my neck are drenched as I blow my nose on one and wipe my eyes on the other. I'm a snotty, bloody mess and I don't care. I'm getting lost in it.

What he does then changes everything. Taking both my hands in his, he kisses them, holding them to his lips, and lets me cry. His simple tender gesture cracks open my heart. It spills all over. I sob. I sob and he simply sits with me until I'm spent. I'm shocked at the depth of this hidden sorrow and his willingness to hold a space for it. I wonder if he knows what a gift he is giving me.

I'm rather adept at finding and expressing my joy. Joy is a more familiar emotion to me, not buried deeply like this concealed minefield I've wandered into. I've made joy my *raison d'être* which in turn has opened a world of wonder, inquiry and pleasure into which I gladly immerse myself. Pleasure is certainly my preference. When I gather the courage to look at him directly, I see now that his worried expression is melting away. He wears a hint of a smile encouraging a shy one from me. I reach to hug him.

"Meu coração agradece." My heart says thank you.

"Estou aqui." I am here. "Now you go. Change some clothes. I cook. We eat with good wine. This is right?"

Oh yes! This is right. The right way to be. The way friends are. We will be friends. I nod affirmatively to him and show him the fish and vegetables I'd purchased for dinner tonight. After producing another bottle of wine, I stumble into my room.

What I see in the mirror is shocking. I am a mess, an absolute mess, and at the same time radiant. Pressure, burdens, deadlines, years, and even pounds seem to have evaporated from my image. I look and feel light, almost translucent. It's magical.

A warm shower calls my name. My wet, blood-stained clothes drop to a pile on the bathroom floor. I should fill the basin with cold water and let them soak but I don't. I want to stand in the warm rain of my shower and wash away any last residue of this unexpected, unspecified sadness. Even though the blessed water stings my scrapes, the pleasure of standing in this delicious deluge cleanses my soul and trumps anything my physicality can dish out. When I finally emerge from the shower I find my skirt and scarf in the basin soaking in cold water.

Wrapped in a soft, white, lavender-scented towel, I glance again at my refection in the mirror. I look different alright. Something more than just the weather has changed. From my open bedroom window I can hear the wild wind whipping branches of the eucalyptus tree against the cottage. Before latching it closed, I notice that most of the brilliant tropical blooms on that huge tree leaning into my courtyard have dropped laying a fragrant pink carpet on my terrace.

But now the aroma of sautéing shallots and the soft pulse of a Latin beat catch my attention and I remember with a startled shiver that Feliciano is in my kitchen. Somehow the incredible sunset rendezvous, the crash and rescue of the last hour have completely slipped my mind which can only mean that I've lost it. I need to find something comfortable and light to wear so I reach for my shell pink dress to slip on. It's a soft jersey, sleeveless and short enough to avoid the raw scrape on my thigh.

There is a beautiful man in the next room and yet here I stand before my mirror again examining myself curiously, without a shred of vanity. That observation alone is notable. I am a sensual woman. I enjoy making an effort to look my best. I do this for myself, but if there is a man on my radar vanity will surely rule. I feel so peaceful, transported after this unexpected tear-drenched catharsis. Untangling my hair and applying a little pale pink lipstick is all I can manage at the moment. I am transfixed by the unfamiliar image of myself in the mirror. Then I notice Feliciano in the doorway watching me. How long has he been standing there?

"Bela." He says. It's almost a whisper. Beautiful. Who is this sensitive young man who suddenly arrived with the wind? I watch him watch me and try to make sense of the events leading to this moment. His aura is calm, a soothing presence grounded in a feeling of antiquity. "I concern. No. I mean. Umm. I worry. You okay?"

Am I? I feel funny but strangely more okay than ever. "Yes, I am very okay, thanks to you for your kindness and good care." He continues to stand motionless, almost without expression. Did he understand what I just said? This is how confounding communicating with language is. It's nearly impossible if both speak the same tongue but it's a damn Tower of Babel miracle if communication manages to occur in two languages.

He walks back into the kitchen only a few steps away, returning in an instant with a chilled glass of wine. He hands me the glass and takes my other hand leading me to the table. I can't believe it! The table is set beautifully with a candle, a single freesia in a pot from my terrace garden, and two plates of simple elegantly prepared food. I am in heaven. And I realize suddenly that I'm ravenous. He pulls out the chair for me. I could get used to this. The pleasure of that thought jars me back into a self-conscious, here-and-now awareness of his hand on my shoulder. The ease with which he slides into the chair across from me at this small bistro table, his intense dark eyes fixed on mine, his parted lips are impossible to ignore.

"*Você come.*" Eat. He gestures with his hand to my plate. He is serious. Still in caretaking mode and gorgeous.

"Gorgeous." I don't realize I've spoken out loud until I see him smile and remember he likes this word. "Gorgeous, Feliciano!" And I mean it. I mean beyond beautiful, delicious, wonderful, fabulous. I mean him, the table, the food, the moment, the way I feel, the good fortune that arrived on that wild wind from Africa. As if choreographed, we clink our wine glasses and sip the moment with our eyes before our lips touch the glass. Lifting our forks in tandem, we savor the mouthwatering fare. It's a luscious, slow, sensuous dance.

"Fabulous!" He looks at me quizzically sifting through his mental translator to discern the meaning of this word. "Fabulous Feliciano. Wonderful, gorgeous, delicious, yummy." He understands now and we laugh.

"Now you are happy, *Senhora* Savannah?"

"Yes, *Senhor* Feliciano. I am happy beyond words." How do I express to him in the familiar? Our formal salutations don't fit now but I don't really know the customs. "Do you have a nick name?" He shrugs, unfamiliar with that term. "A short name, a name of affection, a name your friends call you?"

"Oh. *Sim.* My friends call my name, Chano."

"May I? We're friends now so no need for *Senhora*. Okay?"

"Yes, we use our friend names. What yours is?"

"Just Savannah. That's all."

"Okay, just Savannah." He winks. It's adorable.

He takes my hand and kisses it. So natural and unaffected. It's not at all like he's flirting or coming onto me. It's more a friendly affection. It must be cultural; it's so unusual and refreshing. I would really like to get used to it. And he cooks. The fish is perfectly done, mildly seasoned with shallots and *tempero baiano*, flavorful, not too spicy. A chopped kale salad with orange wedges and a light citrus dressing is the perfect compliment. I had set some black beans to soak for *feijoada*, but they aren't ready to be cooked yet and won't be traditional anyway since I dislike pork. Maybe *gorgeous* Chano will show me the right spices to start them tomorrow. Oh, I hope there is a tomorrow.

"A toast to you, my new friend and hero. Thank you for taking such fine care of me." I lift my glass to his again. We lock eyes as we drink. He says nothing. I don't know how to back up and translate anyway so am content to enjoy the lack of banter in this moment.

But he surprises me with, "This is *my* pleasure, my new friend, Savannah. Come with me in morning to fish. You give good luck. We catch your fish."

I feel as though a song has just been sung for me alone. He'll take me fishing! Sitting across from him now, I can think of only one thing I'd rather do more than fish with him in the morning and that is wake up with him in the morning. But this will not happen. Why? I'm certain he won't make that overt move; there is nothing in his behavior that suggests it and I have decided not to lead. Everything is different with him.

Outside a gale is howling. The windows bang against the sills. The French doors opening onto the terrace slam shut with a force that rattles our glasses. Feliciano jumps up to secure them. I gather the notes and papers that have scattered over the floor. A vase of orange blossoms shatters on the tile. The candle on our little table blows out and so does the power. Silky darkness immobilizes me.

I am barefoot near broken glass. I see nothing but a vague denseness, the shape of Feliciano across the room.

"*Merda . . . merda.*" Shit. He curses under his breath "Savannah. No move."

His sandals crunch over the broken glass on the tiles as he approaches me. Unable to see, we sense the nearness of each other at the same moment. I am in an altered state. The practical things I ought to be considering—like where are the matches and why don't I have a flashlight or know where the hell the gas or water valves are located—don't seem to concern me. My eyes begin to adjust to the dark and I realize that Feliciano is facing me, his hands now on my shoulders, his strong presence comforting me, his scent drawing me toward him.

"Be still." He embraces me. His voice calm with assurance, his warm breath soothing on the top of my head, his confidence and authority quell my anxiety.

"I just moved here a short time ago, I don't know where anything is." He can't understand me. Tears again? No, I won't allow it. Whatever has come over me tonight? "There's broken glass." He knows that. What's the point of anything I say now? I rest my head on his chest, overcome with helplessness. I'm weary with it, grateful he can't see. I don't want him to see me so weak. I make a supreme effort and will these damn tears to stop.

"Stay. I light candle."

I reluctantly release him as he pulls away. The candlelight casts eerie shadows across the room. The wind screeches outside, its force overturning what I guess to be several pots on the ledge of the terrace and the tiny table against the palm tree. Branches claw at the cottage. But now I can see him. I can see the shards of glass and water dispersed across the room reflected in the pale glow of the candle and the lovely table of food, colorless now in the dim light. What I can't see is where to step with any certainty or safety and I can't seem to muster a single word to assist Feliciano—Chano—in determining what to do next.

For a moment he too seems unsure of options. *"Merda, mer-da, merda,"* is what he mumbles, my sentiment exactly. "Where your shoe?"

I'm forced to admit that I have no idea where I kicked them off, probably on the terrace. My feather light slippers have likely been blown into the Amazon by now. Chano (I'm not so sure I can adapt to this *friendly* name. Feliciano is so much more beautiful and meaningful.) steps close and swoops me into his arms, depositing me onto my bed in a swift, fluid, effortless motion. Thick darkness surrounds me once again until he returns with the single candle, placing it on the small table next to my bed. He sits down close to me, his hand carelessly on my knee.

The roaring storm presses in on my tiny trembling bungalow and on my raw delicate sensitivity. Finally he asks, "What we do now?" I have no answer for him but deep in my tummy a little giggle is forming. The tense alarm of our situation begins to give way to a sense of comic relief. Here we are sitting close together on my bed just as my secret fantasy desired, our bodies simmering in each other's nearness. I slip my hand under his and start to laugh. Surprised, he turns to me, his expression questioning then dissolving into the contagion of laughter. "You happy woman? You okay now?"

"Yes, I am happy." Yes, I am okay is the simple answer until my breath catches with a wretched thought: Will he leave me now that I am? My heart begins to race in a ridiculous irrational panic. "Do you have to go?" Please, no! Good Lord what is wrong with me? I've weathered many storms. They pass. What's the problem?

"No. I don't go. You need me." I do? I need him? If this is true and I realize that it *is* true, then it flies in the face of my former reality of simply admiring him. I do want him and my feelings are becoming complicated. This realization initiates a not-so-subtle change in my demeanor. "You need me, *sim . . .* yes?" Yes. I do, I do. He has sensed the change. We sit in silence now but for the fierce wind wailing outside this tiny sanctuary.

He slides closer, his thighs against mine, his torso leaning against me. "What we do now, just Savannah?"

"I guess we wait." As if in synch we lay down next to each other holding hands, breathing one breath.

Turning to me, arranging his arm under my neck, pulling me a little closer, taking care that nothing touches the wound on my thigh, he ever so lightly grazes my cheek with his lips and whispers, "Okay. We wait."

The tenderness of his lips and now the calming way his body feels against mine as he breathes so softly takes my mind off the wicked wind thrashing outside. My leg stings something fierce and the scrape on my arm is now begging for attention as well. I strain away from him, peering over my shoulder to peek at my damaged body parts. I shouldn't have. They're both raw and seeing that only accentuates my discomfort. I have to resist the wimpy temptation to feel sorry for myself. I don't have any salve for them anyway, so there is nothing to do but endure it. And I'm so dog-tired from my emotional spending spree that my mind drifts away from my body. I curl into Feliciano's side, falling into his breathing pattern, acutely aware of his pulse, his heart beating, his scent fresh like ocean air.

Then heavy rain begins to batter the tiles on the roof. The storm doesn't bother to ease into it. The pounding of this tropical storm is deafening. I've never experienced anything like it before. Coming recently from the northwest corner of the United States where the rain is more a perpetual drizzle, only now and again an emphatic downpour, I am unprepared for this deluge.

"Is this a hurricane, Chano? Will the roof come off? Should we try to escape?"

I haven't felt worried about the storm till now. Again, I feel as though I've slipped into an altered state. Shouldn't I be concerning myself with some kind of disaster plan? What would it be? I am not yet familiar with these streets, any customs or protocol for evacuations. Unable to master the confusion of my thoughts, my body tenses with dread. I lean in closer to Feliciano and bury my face in his chest.

"No hurricane but streets have flood, we stay, we wait. No fear, we okay." He puts his arms around me now and holds me tight.

Lying in his arms eases my anxiety some and I allow the thunderous torrent of rain to distract me. The candle flickers in the bit of wind stealing in through the long open vents near the ceiling. His energy has changed and though still protective, his breath is different, his vibration more intense. I wonder now if he is telling me the truth about our situation. His body has become tense and alert, almost rigid. Pulling away from him a bit, I want to see his face, look into his eyes. I need to know the truth. His eyes are closed.

"Feliciano, please, tell me the truth. Are we safe here? Should we go? What should we do?" I'm sure he doesn't understand me.

When he opens his eyes I see in them something completely unexpected. He is not afraid at all. His tension is about another matter altogether. He looks longingly into my eyes, disarming me. In the sticky heat I feel him open up to me. His fingers reach up from my neck and become tangled in my hair. His other hand moves slowly down over my back and rests carefully on my bare thigh just above my now forgotten wound. And I understand clearly the message his body is sending. His restrained arousal presses against my legs as he kisses my lips tentatively, tenderly, before pulling away to measure my response.

"I make love with you Savannah. I careful not hurt you. We safe, you safe with me here. Yes?"

I did not sense this coming. This is *always* something I can sense coming. It seems that my wish may be granted. I wanted to fish with Feliciano only slightly more than I wanted to make love with him and wake up next to him. I really wasn't expecting this much delight. My attention is torn between a vigilant awareness of the chaotic storm outside and the increasingly urgent messages my own body is sending me. He kisses me again without reservation and I realize that I want his lips, his hands, his body against mine, inside of mine. My desire overrules the wind and rain. Framing his face in my hands, I reach for his mouth and kiss him, melting with the pleasure of it.

His kiss feels like velvet, tastes like something primal and necessary. I want to search the insides of his lips, his tongue and discover the reason for this abduction of my senses. His velvet lips slip down to ravish my throat as his hand moves around the curve of my hip to the inside of my thigh. Pushing my dress out of his way, his fingers trace the pink line of silk thong I wear. Should his tongue discover that erotic sensitive place, that little valley above my clavicle, I know I will unfold like a flower in time lapse. Instincts guide him; he kisses the spot that undoes me. This place belongs to him now and I involuntarily quiver, offering him my deepest receptivity. His fingers continue their courtship of my thong and slip under the front of my panties, languishing on my mound, caressing my labia before ever so inquisitively and deliberately introducing themselves to my inner sanctum. My thighs fall open.

"Savannah, you *tão linda*." I know this means so beautiful.

"Thank you. I feel so beautiful when you look at me like this."

"*Tão maduro y tão convidativo*," he whispers.

"I don't know the meaning of your words, but your eyes and hands, your lips and tongue share with me a secret message." Looking into his eyes, peering deeply into the window that reveals his mind and heart, I feel him. "What do you want to tell me, you with such beautiful eyes filled with desire?"

He chuckles softly. I realize he understands more English than he feels comfortable speaking. He understood me. "You so ripe, so inviting. That is what I say. That is what I know from you. Yes, I fill with you. You let me know you. I desire all you."

Feliciano rolls me onto my back and positions himself over me, carefully opening my legs. Running his hands up the insides of my thighs, he lifts my panties mindfully over my scraped thigh and removes them, staring at me as if seeing a naked woman for the first time. He takes a deep breath and whispers something in Portuguese before gently parting my labia. He looks deeply into my eyes now, an appreciative smile spreading across his face and whispers, *"bela bela,"* biting his lower lip.

Then, with one hand, he pulls my scant dress over my head in a flourish, revealing my naked breasts, nipples alert to his advances. As he lowers his head to kiss, to fondle, to caress each one with such tender passion, my vagina begins to pulse, swell and brim with juice. Suddenly I remember the difference in our age, although I don't know exactly how vast that is. I feel self-conscious and exposed. I try to read his expression. He pauses, sensing my tension, gazing at my face cradled now in his strong hands. I close my eyes hoping to avoid exposing my vulnerability. He kisses my lips, my lashes, my ears, my cheeks and tells me again how beautiful, how ripe, how delicious I am. I want to believe he means that, of course, but does he really? Is it true?

"Yes. This is true." He whispers into my ear. He can read my thoughts too? I melt beneath his hands now gently caressing my face. I can't remember the last time I felt such a caring touch, such an exquisite intimacy.

I hunger for his passionate kiss, while I fumble with the buttons of his loose rayon shirt, a pale blue that slides from his body like water. He unzips his grey cargo shorts, worn to a soft finish, and I can't suppress a grin as his precious cargo springs forth revealing what I expertly assess to be perfectly suited for my pleasure. Ignoring the storm wailing through the trees and pummeling my garden, I pull him to me and slide my hands down the inside of his groin feeling the power in his sex. His bronzed skin is a moist patina, the moan deep in his throat quickening my arousal. My sacred chalice is a ready receptacle for him.

He touches me there, first with his fingers, which he tastes in exaggerated appreciation. Now he anchors himself, his hands under my arms lifting my breasts to his mouth. My arms wrap around his neck and my lips seek his ear, but when his cock touches the tip of my clit, I tremble. "Ahhhhh." I feel that lightness of being again, like I did before my mirror a couple hours ago. Am I translucent now? He is down between my legs, his fingers slipping back into my deep, discovering my secrets. His tongue is like silk as it slides the length of my slit. Yes. I see my arms are glowing, it's not my imagination. I begin to gleam, coming long and smooth like moonlight on the ocean stretching across the horizon. My body shimmering with ripples, the natural movements of divine pleasure.

"*O Meu Deus! Encantado!* My God, Savannah, you are enchanting." I float back to shore, to him. But something in the air has changed. We both notice it. Something is different. Several moments pass before we realize what it is. The thundering rain and wild wind have ceased. It's quiet. *"Perfeito!"* he whispers. "Now is perfect time."

I am ready for him. I also have no condoms. How do I say this? I can scarcely find my voice at the moment. "A condom? A life vest?" A deal breaker? I am unprepared. I hadn't planned for this event. But everything I am yearns for his plunge into my depths. I'm about to make a reckless decision.

But he reaches for his shorts and produces a crumpled wrapper containing our life preserver. He smiles, opening it quickly. With a relieved sigh, I roll it over his ready shaft. Pulsing with desire I guide him into me. He makes his way slowly into my channel. I can hear his heart beat in time with mine. He kisses me deeply and swims gracefully into my depths. It takes my breath away. He moves inside of me with such exquisite precision, every particle of me notices. We make love together intuitively finding and recognizing our rhythm, touching and moving as if we've known each other, been learning each other's bodies for years. This rarely happens. Although my body is always pleased to respond sexually, rarely do my deepest emotions feel touched so early in an acquaintance. He is more than an acquaintance.

In one night alone he has touched my heart and soul with his genuine warmth and intimacy. I am almost afraid to think of the dawn. He says I need him. I do. This almost frightens me. I have to put this thought out of my mind.

Feliciano is losing himself. He calls my name. "Yes, yes." He has found me. I can feel him deep inside now, his charged sex slipping over my spot. His ebb and flow coaxing a tidal wave of pleasure, I cry out in ecstasy. He clutches my hips, thrusting him-self into me until he releases the entire contents of his erection, our orgasm long and blissful. We lay vibrating in each other's arms, breathless and filled with joy. Feliciano means happy in Portuguese. He is perfectly named. I am perfectly happy. So who can explain the reason for these tears again?

He feels them on his cheek and lifts his face to mine with an expression of concern yielding to confusion. I am smiling through my tears. I am as confused as he. I shrug and kiss him. "I don't know why."

"You are not happy now?" He is still vibrating inside of me. I am happy beyond words.

"Happy tears of joy, Feliciano. You can see how I feel. I know you can feel me. I can't explain all these tears tonight. They are like the storm that has passed. They are leaving me."

I kiss him and realize I am falling. I hadn't reckoned on this. He lingers in our embrace and holds me so securely, as if he were to let go for even a moment, what we've become might slip away. I am certain he hadn't reckoned on this either. We lay like this, tucked inside each other. "*Eu te adoro*, Savvanah." I adore you. He adores me! Already! We drift to sleep.

When I awaken, my windows are opened to a gentle breeze ushering in the fragrance of bruised flowers. I am lying naked under a corner of the sheet on my bed in this tiny room. My body is deeply rested and deliciously content. I hear Feliciano humming in the kitchen. I smell the coffee and hear the morning noises of this not-quite-posh lane in the Leblon. I am awakening to the memory of beautiful Feliciano touching me with the tip of his tongue. My body begins to respond, my fingers finding the place where his tongue awakened me, recalling him next to me, in me, shielding me from the frightening storm last night. I curl onto my side and come fully awake to a searing pain on the flank of my thigh.

"Oh!"

All the sensations and feelings of last evening flood into my consciousness. Brilliant colors of sunset, raw bloody scrapes on my body, tears and tears, delicious sensual food, the wicked storm, hot sticky darkness, making love, making love. Making love with Feliciano. And now I see him standing, smiling in the doorway. He comes to me, kissing my forehead running his hands from my neck over my breasts to my belly. I laugh as he tousles my tangled mop of hair and reach for him, pulling him into me again. I want him. I need more of him. Instead of succumbing to me, he pulls a tube of ointment from the pocket of his shorts and soothes my stinging wounds, then leaves me in a pre-orgasmic swirl of pleasure. He returns from the kitchen again immediately with a mug of steaming espresso, which he sets on the small table next to my bed. Picking up my pink dress from the floor he dresses me, slipping my panties carefully over my thigh, touching, exploring, teasing my sticky inner workings as he arranges them in place. I want him, I need him. But he steps back from me again, pulls my fingers from the belt loop of his shorts and places the coffee in my hand. Grinning, he kisses me on the cheek, produces his mermaid fishing spool and tucks it in my free hand.

"We come back here soon and love, but now is right time we catch your fish, *meu amante*." My lover.

Feliciano is taking me fishing this morning. He is calling me his lover. Feliciano means happiness. I came to Rio to write this story.

"Dogs are better than human beings because they know but do not tell."
~ Emily Dickinson

The Dog at Her Door

Her name is Savannah. Warm, soft, sweet-scented Savannah. She's the most important person in the world—at least to me. I mean that. Without her, I would be lost and forsaken. She's my whole life and I love her with all my heart. I know she loves me too. But she *makes* love with him.

Maybe you're wondering how I know she loves me so much. Just witness the adoring way she fusses over me, kisses and talks to me, cradles me so tenderly. That should convince you. Plus she tells me how much she loves me all the time. She means it. I can feel it.

But she *makes* love with him.

Wouldn't I do anything for her? I would. She only needs to call me, ask me. It's not as if I'd do silly things like jump through hoops for her, at least not again. Once she dressed me in doll clothes and insisted I roll over and yes, jump through a hula-hoop. She held it close to the floor so I could leap through it and not humiliate myself. I think she understood how embarrassing that was for me since she hasn't insisted that I do it again. I'm grateful for that.

But when she calls me, I come running. I rush to the comfort of her touch and her tangy familiar scent. And I sense her moods. I feel her. I hear her. In the tone of her voice, the expression on her face, the look in her eyes, the way she stands, I know exactly what to expect and how she wants me to be. I know her better than anyone else. I love her.

But she *makes* love with him.

Although that man tries to be friendly with me, he's disingenuous. He doesn't care for me at all. I even heard him tell her that he thought I smelled. Ridiculous! I've been bathed! I'm always well groomed. And she's explained how close we are, how important I am to her. She's been quite clear that our friendship and affection is something he must accept if he wants to spend time with her. We both vie for her attention. It is not amusing.

She greets him at the door with familiar happy sounds that are usually meant for me. I can see how happy he is to see her when she hugs and smothers him in kisses. I know exactly how he feels. She greets me that way too. He doesn't understand that she belongs to me. He tries to ignore me, scarcely hiding his annoyance. He acts as though he wishes I'd just disappear. Still, I am welcoming and friendly. I interact with him as graciously as I can. I'm naturally welcoming to her guests. But when he's here, she's distracted. Sometimes I have to beg her to notice me, take care of me, pet me, feed me. She always does so lovingly.

But she makes love with him.

I never know for sure what they're going to do so I pay keen attention to their every move. Sometimes they just sit and talk. She nuzzles close to him on the sofa. I've learned I must position myself just near enough so she won't tell me to move or push me away. He's always kissing and touching her. She kisses him back—ignoring me, never wondering how that makes me feel. I watch and wait, trying not to be intrusive. I know better than to beg for her attention when he's here.

She *wants to make* love with him.

They spend time in the kitchen talking and laughing, cooking, tempting me with wonderful, irresistible smells. She offers him the tastiest samples. He licks her fingers. It's too much to bear. I nudge her leg. *Hey, Savannah! I'm still here.* When she gives me a morsel and I lick her fingers too, she shoos me out of the kitchen and washes her hands. I feel pathetic when she laughs about how I'm always underfoot. Then they sit at the table after dinner for a long time discussing things I seldom understand, having tedious conversations that lull me to sleep. She's okay that I'm curled at her feet but when he's here, I'm reduced to sitting on the sideline of her attention.

She wants him to *make* love with her.

I follow them into our bedroom. He's the one to lie close to her, touch her, relish her kisses on his neck, his ear. He's the one she caresses. He's the one groaning with pleasure, not me.

She's going to *make* love with him.

And they forget completely that I'm with them too, even as I curl up in my spot by the door pretending to sleep. I watch. Doesn't she realize that I can hear them and see them? Doesn't she realize that I watch how he undresses her and lets her clothes drop to the floor at their feet? He pets her, running his hands along her body. Sometimes I get the feeling he does this to taunt me. He'll look directly at me with an odd smile, a certain look in his eye. I don't dare come closer.

Once she scolded me harshly in front of him when she caught me chewing on her panties. I just wanted to keep her sweet mysterious scent close to me. He laughed. He stokes her soft skin and she smiles, her warm breath whispering to him not me. The bed creaks when he moves close to her. Shouldn't I be the one lying next to her on *our* bed? He's in my spot!

He's going to *make* love with her.

But he doesn't know her like I do. She has secrets only I know. When he's not here, she likes to play with toys. She tosses me our fetch ball and tickles my tummy with my soft squeaky toy. She plays with her own toys too. Sometimes she crawls under her covers and spends lots of time tickling herself with her favorite toy.

Other times, like after her bath, she forgets about me and I watch her lay back down on top of our bed. She closes her eyes, moves and moans while that funny toy buzzes inside that place between her legs that holds her scent. She gets annoyed and tells me to go get my own toys and leave her alone if I try to jump on the bed. I want her to play with me. I want to play with her toys.

Once she turned off her buzzing toy and left it on her bed while she dressed. I snatched it in my mouth and ran through the house. She caught and scolded me but not before I could taste her scent on it. I only wanted to chew it for a little while. I could show him where her toys are, but I won't. I will keep her secrets from him. He and I are not friends.

He *makes* love with her.

There is a scent they make together when their clothes are off and they have been playing and rolling around on our bed for a while. Their scent together is different than just hers, or just his. Something excites me about that scent, reminding me of something I can't quite remember. He lays his naked body on top of her, touching and licking that one place that sends her scent. Once when she finished with her toy I tried to lick her scent there too and she slapped me hard and shoved me away from her. She was cruel to me. Why wouldn't she allow me to do that if he does?

With him she makes soft sounds. When they start to move together, they make new sounds. I lay near the doorway watching, trying to understand what the sounds mean. I can't bring myself to turn away. Their sounds and their scent intrigue me. I have to watch and listen.

This is how they *make* love.

I hear her moan. I hear him groan. What has happened? He stops moving over her. Is she hurt, did he hurt her? I stand and listen. I go to her. I need to protect her. But I see that her eyes are shining and she is holding him close, kissing him. I hear her telling him that she loves him. I can't believe what I'm hearing. That can't be true! That's a lie! She loves me. She has told me so my whole life. But he believes her lie. He kisses her back and holds her closer. He is happy. I am not.

I wait for her to notice me and tell him she doesn't mean what she said to him. Tell me again that I am the one she loves. I need to remind her about that with what she refers to as my adorable little *yip yip*. But she tells me, "Shhhh!" My heart is crushed when she scolds me and evaporates when she ignores me. I scarcely exist to her when he is here.

They make love together.

Tomorrow, in the afternoon, she will tell her girlfriend all about him. She will talk on the phone a long time about how he made her feel. I will hear her describe what they did. I have no idea what her words mean. Never has she explained to me about these things. She has never once asked me how I feel about him. She doesn't even seem to notice how alone I feel when he takes her attention away from me. She giggles when she tells her girl-friend about what he says to her, how he touches her.

How she loves it when they are *making* love.

She will not mention the fact that I was there watching. She will not mention me at all. But here is my solace: I will be here with her tomorrow afternoon and every night and he will not. I am the one who rides in her car, sits at her feet as she works, and takes her on long walks. I am the one she strokes and pets and feeds every day. I am the one she truly loves.

She only *makes* love with him.

C'est si bon
Lovers say that in France
When they thrill to romance
It means that it's so good.
  ~ Henri Betti and André Hornez, 1947

C'est Si Bon!

My Luc, that charming *bon vivant*, is an exaggerated example of French flamboyance with his accent still as thick as a round of triple cream Brie. By design, he appears in perpetual need of a haircut. And with those hand painted silk scarves draped carelessly around his neck, a cigarette dangling from his lips, maybe always just a little drunk, you can be sure that wherever he is, there's music and color, romance and pleasure. Living and making art here on the southern California coast for over 35 years, he's managed to remain quintessentially and stereotypically French, and it's worked well for him.

We met by chance, through a mutual friend, at which point he immediately and persistently began to woo me. He was quite impossible to resist. I'd discover love notes like this one slipped under my door in the early mornings:

Wandering breathlessly over the welcoming Savannah
Face down between horizons of dawn and dusk
A mound of soft warm sweet grass fragrant on my cheek
Thirst quenched by her precious dew
I survive another day.

Or perhaps I'd find flowers or chocolate or a warm brioche. My portrait once appeared, painted on a scallop shell and wrapped in one of his scarves. Strolling on the beach at sunset last spring, he placed a vintage gold locket filled with mysterious fragrant herbs around my neck. Ever since, I've worn it as a treasured talisman dangling from a delicate chain nestled between my breasts, its patina against my skin reminding me of him.

Wherever Luc finds himself, art is created. In the kitchen, sumptuous meals, as simple as a wink or elaborate as a French kiss, are prepared for guests and more often just for me. Lounging on the patio, he may lift my foot to his lap and paint my toenails in intricate designs. He'll drape me in a handmade silk dress from some obscure shop we've chanced upon, then stop me mid-motion to sketch or photograph me as we stroll along the esplanade. Luc tells me I'm a precious gem, a work of art, a masterpiece, and he makes me feel as though I'm a rare and beautiful gift to him. You can imagine why I fell hopelessly, madly in love with him, craving his touch and attention every second.

"Savannah, are your dreamy green eyes open on this beautiful morning? But now I see you are pouting. Stay right here in our bed, *cherie*. I'll bring you a coffee."

This is simply how he is. He awakens this way—alive, engaged, cheerful, in our bed now. On this morning, I awoke with a little champagne headache—nothing at all—and still he tends to me as though he were my personal manservant. He plumps my pillows, brings me some chilled mineral water with a twist of lemon. Then he reappears with an espresso on a tray decorated with sprigs of lavender, a small dish of raspberries, and the paper before slipping back in bed next to me. Lying together, sipping and reading, he enthusiastically shares gossip about someone or something from the Arts and Entertainment section, while I devour the local and world news which is of no interest to him at all. We have the luxury of our leisure at this time. This luxury is an unprecedented and delicious experience for me, a woman who has known nothing but work and encumbrance for most of her life.

"What are you doing today, lover? Tell me your plans and I'll tell you mine," I say, still sleepy, not really planning anything.

"We have not yet made love this morning so I have not tasted your lips or breasts. This is my only plan. I was dreaming of your ankles so I think these are where to kiss you first."

He sets our cups on the table, and dives under the quilt popping out the other end to lay his cheeks on my ankles. His careless chin stubble makes me laugh. He's always surprising me with his eccentric passions. Never can I predict what Luc will do next. He is spontaneous and outlandish and spends lavish amounts of time and energy tending to my whims and making love to me. Deliciously. Sometimes he is slow and sensuous, others frenetic and ravishing. This morning he's taken with my ankles and calves, massaging and kissing before crawling up my torso to my neck and lips.

Is it his *savoir faire* or is it because he is an artist that the beauty, form, and moods of a woman intrigue him? He makes love like he makes art. I become his canvas, his fingers outlining patterns, his lips and tongue filling in depths of chiaroscuro. He tastes me, describing my flavors in whispers of color and texture. Losing himself in a subtle kiss, he takes me with him to hidden pleasures. When he caresses me, I become warm clay, seductively shaped and molded to his desires. And when he opens and enters me, I swear to heaven that I not only hear but feel vibrations and tones of music coming from him as if he were tuning his instrument to me in perfect pitch and harmony. Every morning is a new creation, each day a work in progress.

The morning is young for us although it's nearly noon. I'm ready to get on with the day. "Brunch?" I ask him. "I'm starving." I roll over him and head for the shower.

"Until I have tasted your sweet juices, nothing will I eat or drink."

I hear him mumble absently. I glance over my shoulder at him muttering in French about an installation opening in one of the local galleries this week. "Would you consider a mimosa and omelet instead?" It's not that I don't love our sensual morning sessions, I do. But just now, after a night of indulgences, I'd rather let warm water wash over me and clear my head.

"You've tempted me with champagne, so now I cut some herbs to make you an herb omelet. But first our shower, *cherie. C'est si bon.*"

Standing in our outdoor shower, secluded by the tall lush bamboo that surrounds our terrace, he washes me lovingly from head to toe, finger painting in the lather, cooing his appreciation as I shampoo his long hair and massage his scalp. He leaves me alone to languish in the pleasure of the warm water. I watch him wrap himself in my vintage silk kimono, a lit Gitane cigarette already hanging from his lips. He turns on some John Coltrane and strolls into the kitchen. I dry my hair in the sun until he returns with fresh pressed mimosas and a soft herbed cheese omelet. We kiss and toast another beautiful morning. This magical life! A romance story I can't seem to put down on paper, and why not? Isn't that currently my only vocation? Hasn't he given me both the luxury of support and time? Doesn't he provide me with ample material for a romance novel? Indeed. But I just can't do it.

"So Luc, what are your plans today?" No answer. A quiet day, maybe writing in the garden, staying in today sounds just right for me. "Hey! What are you doing today?" No answer. "Later I could check on your mother and bring her some croissants for tea. If I'm inspired I can see what's fresh in the market for our dinner tonight." I wander into his study in search of a response. "Shall I meet you at the bistro this afternoon for a glass of wine?" I discover him hunched over his phone engrossed in rapid texting. When I come close, he turns it off and throws it carelessly onto a mess of paperwork on his desk.

"*Oui.* We will meet at the bistro, at four, I think is good. I will go to my studio and paint until then. Perhaps we visit the new boutique that is open now next to the bistro."

He loves to shop for me, dress me, decorate and adorn me. We are living in a paradise we recreate each morning, never discussing, considering or acknowledging the possibility that our fairy tale life could be temporary or ever end. This thought only surfaces for me as a nightmare, something I push far away when it dares to appear.

Have I had doubts about Luc and his ability to commit himself to just one woman, in particular, me? Yes, almost daily. I've stopped myself from peeking into his phone's call and text history. I've admonished myself not to surprise him at his studio, again. I did once and discovered he was out. I called him. No answer. I called him a number of times. Nothing.

Later when I asked him about his day and who he happened to see, he said, "I painted all day and saw no one of any interest." Really? When I mentioned as casually as I could manage, that I'd come by and found him gone and the shop locked, there was no comment from him.

"No explanation? I was just wondering, that's all," I tossed out offhandedly. He didn't bite. He had no explanation and no response at all. He merely stared into my eyes and I felt as if he were daring me to reveal my insecurity. It was then I noticed for the first time, a line. When had it been drawn? Who is drawing it now? I let my mind spin over several miserable, unsavory presumptions all featuring him with another woman. "That" other woman, the one he threw over for me.

Celia is her name and she is a dark beauty. Also French, and like him, long since settled in Laguna, long gone from France. I've quizzed him before about Celia. Early in our love affair he was more willing to talk about her as a former. We were both drawn to share our other love stories and dreamily conclude that to ours, nothing compares. That was only a second ago to me, a long two-year second. Somewhere along this year, Luc no longer wished to share those stories, claiming all had been said. He declared it being our job now to live and love fully and contentedly. No argument from me there. But at the same time I do not agree. In regard to the importance I place on sharing every intimate detail of our life together, I don't believe all has been said. Or perhaps it's simply my addiction to needing no barriers between us. What the evolving parameters now entail I'm not only afraid to guess, I'm reluctant to know.

Isn't it true in any relationship that the exciting wonder of exploring it with someone new in time blends into something known, then something understood, then something on the dangerous side of complacent? There's that wretched moment when one comprehends deeply that the first wedge has found its way into the tender fleshy membrane we've become, that fragile envelope we've secured ourselves within. This acknowledgement gives me pause and triggers a reminder of what it is to mourn, because this outer layer of protection called trust is the first to succumb. I've discovered, through error mostly, that how I handle the first breach of any belief or trust sets up a dynamic and precedent for the next one—and there will be a next one.

Luc has given me no real reason to mistrust him. And often I must remind myself that I am not absolutely certain what the actual nature of our union now is or what its assumed future might become. We're relatively new and still in love. I definitely am anyway, and this depth of feeling makes me all the more vulnerable to the mere idea of losing that most coveted experience in life.

But nevertheless, returning now to what I am grateful for, reestablishing order, growing up and carrying on: What I love most about Luc is his presence. He is completely present when he is with me. He gives his attention fully to me, to what I have to say, to what I might be feeling, to what I might be needing, to what I don't even realize wants or needs attention. He is sensitive and imaginative, commanding and gentle, authoritative and yielding, masterful and patient. He acts as if the world revolves around me alone. It may well be an act; it likely is. I don't like to think that, but if it's true, then he has perfected his part. He's had plenty of practice. He is a fantastic and adoring lover, making love to me as if it is the most important work of his life. Luc makes everything a celebration, an event. Yes, he's simply this way and completely impossible to resist. Why bother trying? My fate is sealed with his, whatever the fates allow.

But do I work on the myriad of stories my mind conjures? I do, and more than I'd like to think is warranted. In fact, the disturbing pictures that my overactive imagination projects from my mind are the only things to find themselves written on the page lately. I still cannot accurately and honestly articulate loving Luc. So for now, I release myself from the self-inflicted torture that has threatened to become my familiar.

Later in the afternoon, when I meet him on the balcony of our favorite bistro overlooking Laguna Beach, he jumps up excitedly to embrace me. My sordid interpretations of unsubstantiated impressions are abandoned for now and slip into the recesses of deep memory.

"I have a wonderful surprise for you, *cherie*. Close your eyes for just a minute and take my hand. Let me lead you." I hesitate. I want to comply but feel unsteady and a bit dizzy closing my eyes on this high balcony. "Close your eyes! Let me show you something spectacular." I sense the railing and grasp it to secure myself. "And now you may open your eyes. Look!"

I open my eyes to reveal a table set with a single pink peony I recognize he's picked from the garden next to his studio. A bottle of Veuve Clicquot chills in a bucket. Grilled oysters and leeks, warm French bread, and herbed butter accompany a view of the Pacific Ocean with the sun falling from an orange and magenta sky. "Oh my goodness!" I sigh. How surreal the colors of the sky are this afternoon and superimposed, as if painted over this drapery of pigment and tone, a sleek and magnificent yacht is slowly making its way northward like a mirage on a shimmering ocean amid soft warm breezes.

"How divine, lover, what a beautiful still life." Once again, I feel as if he has painted a masterpiece for me alone. I reach to kiss him. His smoky breath, which on anyone else would be repugnant, is always somehow sweet and seductive. His nose nestles into my cleavage, nuzzling the golden locket.

"What I wish to point out to you, *cher*, is this vessel. See, she is now making a lazy progress up the coast but later she will dock in Newport. When she does, we will drive to meet her and take an overnight voyage with my friend, the seafarer captain. He invites us to join him."

"Oh! Magnificent!" I squeal. This is naturally a welcome and delightful respite to my frame of mind just hours ago. And so you see, just when I waver dangerously near the edge of our understanding, he bursts forth with assurances like this one leaving no room at the inn for self-sadism. "Shall I run to the house and pack some things? I can be quick." I ask impulsively. I wonder where we are going and what we will need. It's my nature to plan for contingencies and I have a long, sometimes stoic, history of doing so.

"I have seen to everything, Savannah, *belle femme*," he cooed. "We have all we need to enjoy making love under the stars. But now, let's taste these oysters and toast our sea voyage with champagne. I'll fondle your thighs in secret under the table and you can imagine the many ways I will enchant you on the top deck with only the moon as our witness."

We sat close, quietly, with our arms around each other, watching the sun fall into the ocean. At times I have felt that this is not really my life. Now was one of those times. Sitting here with him, about to embark on such a romantic cruise, is a storybook fairy tale. I'm still not completely used to the kind of loving and lavish consideration he extends to me and I'm almost afraid to become accustomed. These are the moments when my life feels so mythical that I have to pinch myself to be certain that I'm not dreaming, watching a movie, lost in a romance novel, or dead and already in heaven.

His phone buzzes. He glances at it and quickly shoves it in his pocket. It buzzes again. He ignores it; I can't. Minutes later he excuses himself to use the restroom. Does he think I can't see through this ruse? I'm immediately thrust back into morose suspicions and the gamut of feelings from despondent reflections to sublime bliss and back to morose debilitation is wearing on me. I'd no sooner convinced myself that this morning's frenetic secretive texting was to arrange this afternoon's lovely surprise when the wicked lead weight of dread descended upon me again. He's been gone now longer than it takes to piss, hasn't he? How long? And then he's back with his arm around my shoulders as if nothing untoward has occurred. And nothing has. I make myself crazy.

"Who was that, darling?" I strive to assume a careless, even casual, tone to defray my angst from his attention.

"Who was who?" he answers absently pulling a piece of the sweet yeasty bread from a small loaf and smearing it with savory butter.

I sense his evasion. I don't want to ruin his plans for our special evening cruise with my fears. I don't want to ruin the moment. Also I sense the futility of prying, pressing him to tell me his business or worse, force him to fabricate some tale I won't be able to confirm. I want to be in love. I am in love with Luc. The caveat is that I want him all to myself. I'm not the open, sharing kind when it comes to us. Not when it comes to another woman. He knows that. He is also, as I've mentioned, French. And so is Celia. And although he never mentions her, I could draw a line here and force the issue. It won't serve me, this I know. And look how he has gone out of his way to make me happy and give me pleasure. I make a decided effort to file my emotions. It is entirely possible that he got a text from a gallery, a friend, his mother . . . I have to stop torturing myself.

"Oh, I just meant I heard a text come through on your phone and wondered is all." I reach for my champagne flute and linger over a small sip. It's my favorite and I'm sure it's as delicious as always but I can't seem to taste it at the moment. What will it take to divest myself of this dark cloud hanging over my mood?

"Nothing important. Nothing I can't attend to tomorrow." He smiles and winks. He winks? This gesture is unexpected and disarming and it's out of character. I've never seen him wink before and it serves to heighten my suspicions.

"Hmmmm," I murmur.

"Can you just imagine how the sea and stars will caress us tonight?" He takes my fingers and brings them to his lips, kissing each tenderly. "Our love deserves this little journey. We deserve every pleasure in our lives." He has sensed my internal inquiry and tension. "I hope you feel the same, *cherie.*"

I discover I've been holding my breath and now release a long sigh before taking another sip of champagne. I shouldn't have to work at trusting this man I care for so deeply. He has truly done nothing but show me love and affection in ways I've never experienced before. Maybe that is exactly my problem. I'm wielding a magnifying glass like a weapon, searching for a fissure that will prove I'm right; that a wedge has found its way in to crack apart my foundation of faith. This is my issue, my pathos. It's not his and never would be. I stop myself yet again from ruining my own life with my own thoughts. Pathos indeed.

We board the yacht in the twilight, and after we leave the port, the warm evening breeze and gentle rolling of the ocean lulls us into a trancelike state. We lay next to each other on an oversized lounge, sipping more champagne, nibbling on strawberries and almonds, and cruising toward Avalon on Santa Catalina Island. I feel much relieved, more secure. Champagne can work magic for unreasonable (or not) distractions. It's the perfect accompaniment for what is beautiful and blissful and in the moment.

"*Cherie,* kiss me," he whispers. "I want to feel your ripe lips on mine. This sliver of moonlight on your cheek inflames me. The rhythm of the sea suggests to me how your body moves like the ocean and I am longing to sink, to feel you pull me deep inside of you, like the moon pulls the tide. When your hips roll with this rhythm, when you come, I will break like waves long against the shore. I can imagine no finer place to be than wrapped within your thighs. I need you, Savannah. I need to taste your sweet salty juices, touch you, and sense you yield to me."

This romantic poetry, these lyrics are how he expresses himself to me. A little dizzy from sipping champagne all afternoon and evening, I'm drifting on the waves, lulled into a reverie, listening to his hypnotic seduction, until he kisses my lips softly. His inquisitive fingers seek the heat hidden between my thighs, as if making that discovery for the first time and I yield to him in appreciation. He kisses my neck, slipping the strap of my dress over my shoulder exposing my breast. I open his shorts. His penis lurches and stiffens with my touch.

The captain has long since gone to the wheelhouse below and we are alone on the top deck of this glamorous yacht, with the beauty of the Pacific Ocean surrounding us, the stars our only company. "*Mon Dieu! Je t'adore*," he whispers in my ear. "*Cherie*, let me taste of you." Lifting my skirt, he expertly moves my thong aside, runs his tongue the length of my crevice, rousing me out of my dreaminess, every cell in my body coming to full attention.

When he feasts on me like this, it's as though he is savoring the finest wine, the rarest truffle, the most exquisite caviar. He's never in a hurry dining on me the way he dines at table, sensuously, slowly with appreciation. If I come, he tells me that I am more delectable than the most rich and delicate sauce he can imagine. I always come. His finger inside of me, gently stroking me while his lips and tongue nibble and lick my clitoris is an existential prelude to my building climax.

Tonight we move slowly, deliciously until I am adrift at sea, yet still aware of my anchor to him. Lifting himself over me and slowly entering, he fills me with his erect sex. God has custom made us to fit congenitally. My head rolls back, my mouth opens in ecstasy, he fills it with his tongue, kisses my throat, cradling my head, burying his face in my hair, his hushed silky breath a soft breeze in my ear.

"Ah, Savannah, how you move me. I could die in this moment with the assurance that God has blessed me. I could live forever in these moments to know it is my life's purpose of serving your pleasure I fulfill. I want to spill myself endlessly into you, cherie. Are you ready to receive me now?"

"Luc, oh yes, now . . . always." He thrusts himself into me, plunging deep into my willingness, our energies and essence a powerful merging, an expansive wave simultaneously flowing out across the ocean and into the depth of our beings. He moves within me the same way he does everything else in his life, fully and completely in the moment, in the design, in the flavors, in sensuous enjoyment of every nuance.

We make love. We make love with a passion that's destined, our sex like the magic of music created spontaneously from the heart. We come together like a long-awaited miracle, like we had been lost and finally found. When we crescendo, it doesn't end. This must be a preview of heaven. We are living and loving in a paradise we have created together. My heart is blessed. I bless him.

I was programmed as a child and learned to believe through the events of my life that all good things must come to an end. That instilled instinct is what has threatened my happiness and contentment throughout my life. Luc tells me this idea is not one that God would consider useful, as there is no reason for good things to come to an end. For now, for tonight, with him, because of him I am learning to accept the goodness and pleasures as they come and consciously build a strong barrier to protect us from that conditioning, All my fears that rise up from the past to cloud my perceptions and all my anxiety of what could go wrong in the future doesn't advance me an inch in this moment. Come what may, this moment is our life. To be lived in joyful appreciation and acceptance of what we are given to possess and share. And for this glorious moment I choose to believe as he does because *mais oui, c'est si bon.*

Eyes. Those damn eyes fucked me forever.
We made love just looking at them.
  ~ Charles Bukowski

His Damn Eyes

I think of myself as an independent woman. I can do what I want. I'm in complete control. I can take care of myself. Do I enjoy the company of a man? Without question, but I'm all right alone. That is until I see him again. Logic tells me to steer clear of him, and I've made concerted efforts, but my heart betrays me. He's not a man I'd choose for a mate. I know better than to expect any sentiment of that nature from him. I don't appear able to expect any sentiment of that nature from myself. I've performed rituals to rid myself of his mastery over me. They work well. That is, until I see him again. He pulls me back. Every time. It's madness.

He drops by unannounced. He gives me that look. A look with which I am agonizingly familiar. I know that look and I know what it means, but it doesn't matter. I fall completely under his spell. It's his damn eyes.

What is it about his eyes? They aren't remarkable; they're hardly beautiful or even memorable. If you looked closely at him you'd likely wonder what the hell is so compelling about his eyes. They're a cloudy sky gray and slightly too wide apart. Bushy eyebrows hang low over them. Maybe it's his habit of peering from the corner of them, as if not addressing his subject directly. Yet even with his head turned just so, his smiling eyes lock on to mine and bore deep past any resistance.

When he's gone, I can step back and give myself a good talking-to, a stern reprimand. I remind myself again and again that he is a narcotic for me and I do quite well without him. I do infinitely better without him. I might feel proud that I've made it possibly thirty-six or more hours and not thought of him once. Then he comes back.

This time will be different, I say. I will not play the fool for him. No more. I absolutely mean this for the sake of my heart and my soul. But then I open the door and let him in. And even though I am painfully aware of how dangerous it is for me to test my resolve like this—to test my strength, to test my faith—all that is only rhetoric. Empty rhetoric. Because once he gives me that sidelong glance, once he smiles and crinkles his damn eyes and gives me that look, it takes my breath away. I become an amnesiac. I am still a skilled, intelligent woman except when it comes to him and his goddamn eyes.

He strolls in like a familiar. He takes my hand, pulls me to him, and calls me baby. I tell him unequivocally that he has to go. Now. I have plans. I'm leaving. He can't stay. Not this time, no, not ever again. But it's always the same. His smile and his damn eyes make me fall in love all over again. And then without fail all my illusions of independence evaporate. I become his personal possession. He not only expects this; he takes it for granted. He's careless with me. But in his fucked-up way, I think he does love me. And I love him. But wait! How can I even entertain that thought? How can I possibly say he loves me? How can I possibly say that I love him? How in any form is this love? If, somehow, it fits any definition of love at all it must be one motherfucking crazy love.

At issue is the case that we are both good and not good together. It is my assertion that we are not good for each other. While the good is just so exquisitely good it cannot be resisted, the not-so-good is abjectly wretched. Where is the balance in this? There is none. So how can this be love? He said he thinks I'm crazy and he loves that, but it's not true, either part. I am not crazy. Not until I am with him and he makes me so. And no matter what I want to think, it's not that he loves me. I am clear that he merely relishes the power he has over me. This is where amnesia slips between the sighs.

And he lies. He is skilled at it. I am so finely tuned to every nuance of expression in his damn eyes that I know when he lies to me. I know it, but so what? Because he is a narcotic to me. He makes everything feel all right. Isn't a drug addict completely aware that their narcotic is harmful? And yet all that matters is feeling that rush, that smooth oblivion? Feeling like that takes precedence over any other desire. I'll never need to resort to drugs. I'm already lost in his damn eyes.

Without touching me, his damn eyes pierce me deeply. They reveal and unnerve me, unclothe, molest, and penetrate me. His damn eyes alone can do that. I detest admitting this, but we both know it's true. And what effect do I have on him? That is an excellent question. I have asked myself this question on innumerable occasions. I come up with no answer. I seem to have no lasting effect on him.

I've challenged him on the dubious importance I seem to have in his life. He points out that he's here, right now, with me. Doesn't he come back again and again? That has to count for something. There must be a compelling reason, he'll say. But what is it, I ask? He says it's crazy love; nothing and nobody else compares. He says it's not just sex. He has sex with other women. I detest hearing this even though I have sex with other men. He says it must be love that we make together. He says he feels at home inside of me. He always comes home. Isn't that love, he asks? So what if it's crazy fucking love? He believes that's as close as the two of us will likely ever get. What a heartbreaking thought. It's heartbreaking because I believe it's true.

So I let him come home again and when does, he's loving and attentive. He begins to relax and feel at ease. But as soon as I follow his lead and let down my guard, as soon as I start playing house, as soon as he's content, as soon as he's had his fill of eating in, he finds a reason to hit the rowdy road. It's his damn eyes. They roam.

He leaves me. He abruptly abandons our home and hope crumbles around me like adobe in an earthquake. He never notices. He's already gone. How compelling for him is our crazy love, really?

Don't even ask me how I feel. Each time I awaken to find he's gone is traumatic, a rude slap across the face. I hunger for his presence until the acutely numb vacancy he leaves inside me begins to recover. I cleanse that space I had once again begun to think of as our home until I can summon the desire and energy to refresh, rebuild, and redecorate. When I finally feel comfortable and able to call the space mine alone, I know I'm healing. I know I'll make it, because one morning I'll awaken and I feel like myself again. I'll look in the mirror and recognize myself. I'll feel like putting on some bright lipstick and starting over.

And what do I think? I have stopped thinking. I have to. Once his energy and memory are smudged out and I am able to invite others to occupy my time and my thoughts—or even to visit that empty space inside of me—I can't let myself think about it. Home is only a place for the two of us.

I say never again and I mean it. I stop thinking about him for days at a time. I'm once again at ease and happy and productive. I've stopped expecting him to call or drop by. I have recreated my life yet again and it's good. I am good.

Then there's a knock at the door. Then, in a cold sweat that floods my resolve, I peek past the chain. He's back. He begs me to let him in. Not this time, no, not ever again! But there he is and he has that look. He calls me baby and begs me to open up and let him come home. I will not play the fool for him. No more. I absolutely mean this even if I'm being redundant. For the sake of my heart and my soul, I do mean it.

He pleads with me, rolling out his familiar excuse, his remorse for hurting me so again and again. My heart is hardened this time. I have gained ground since the last shattering earthquake precipitated by his stealthy exit. He reaches his fingers through the chain and caresses my cheek. I step back. He begs me, please baby please. His damn eyes fill with tears. I close my own eyes so as not to see him. He tells me this time will be different. I say there is no this time and somehow I believe myself. He waits. He tells me he loves me only and wants to come home. This time he means to stay forever. I crack. I open the door to let him in. His eyes cast their spell, turning the key in the lock of my heart. My heart opens up against its will. But I still hand him my only key and he takes it.

It's his damn eyes.

Winter must be cold for those with no warm memories.
  ~ Anonymous

Once In Winter

Miguel stood with the pot of coffee poised over my cup. *"¿Más café, senora?"*

Lost in thought, I hadn't noticed him hovering. *"Ah, sí, gracias, Miguel."*

A small table sits in the corner of a cafe where I like to take breakfast and contemplate my day. The proprietors serve up an air of celebration coupled with the most delightful fresh local cuisine, warmly welcoming both locals and tourists alike. I find this an extraordinarily pleasant way to begin one's day.

One particular morning I lingered because, although I was on holiday, I had some writing to complete in preparation for a talk I would be giving when I returned to the States. I was thinking about the content and gravity of my work as a clinical psychologist over these many years and how more and more I found myself sitting in tedious courtrooms, serving as an expert witness, rather than seeing patients. My mind was wandering, absently observing people as they came through the open front of the café and settled at tables deeper within to escape the already hot and dusty street. It was then that she breezed in.

Several patrons greeted her as she made her way through the crowded café and I was surprised when the owners swooped her up in an embrace of kisses as if they were old friends. In the nearly five years that I've wintered here, I'd never seen her before. I wondered how that could be since she appeared to be quite at home in the café. She chose a table near me. She was altogether lovely.

I watched as she ordered a coffee, fascinated by the subtle way in which the staff and others responded to her, leaning toward her in an attempt to be near. I thought she glanced my way several times, although our eyes never actually met. When I realized that I was staring at her and not too subtly, I picked up my notes and pretended to be occupied with them. At that very moment she looked directly at me with just the hint of an enigmatic smile. Then her attention was captured by a man who stopped to chat with her. I had met him several times before in the café and at events around the village. They were obviously friendly; she kissed him on each cheek, European style, hugging him affectionately before he returned to his table. I wondered again how it was that I hadn't I seen or met her before.

She glanced in my direction several more times and although I wasn't entirely certain she was looking at me, I felt as if her glance might pierce me through if it should happen to land directly. She had a compelling air of casual presence, as though she were at ease in her own body and content to be wherever she found herself. Although she was tanned with no make-up and dressed in a scant sundress, she bore no resemblance in vision or energy to the many young women, with their dreadlocked hair, striving to be free spirits, who found their way to this village hoping to sell their woven necklaces and crocheted bikinis on the beach. Within months many of those dear creatures were seduced and pregnant by some local surfer or waiter, then left to fend for themselves while raising their child on their own.

I studied her profile—the way the bangles on her wrist slid down her arm as she sipped her coffee, how she kept adjusting the strap of her sundress as it slipped off her shoulder. A beaded bracelet on her ankle drew my attention to the firm curve of her calf as she crossed her leg, absently dangling her flip-flop in syncopated time with the ever-present traditional music wafting from the street. We might be close in age, yet watching her I felt suddenly old, out of touch, matronly. I simply could not convince myself to get up to leave even though I'd settled my bill. I accepted several refills of coffee, until I was forced to use the restroom. When I returned, she was gone.

Later the next morning, I was accessing the internet at the outdoor veranda near my rooms at the end of the promenade. I happened to look up just as she strolled by with another couple. She waved and smiled in recognition, as if we'd met. Stunned, I waved in return, but she had already passed, leaving behind a faint luscious scent in her wake. I couldn't think what to do. I had the strongest urge to get up and run after her, to talk with her, to discover where she was staying, to touch her hair. Touch her hair? I hadn't felt this unsettled in decades. Even my body felt strange, unable to assimilate what was happening to it.

The next day went by without my seeing her at the café, on the beach, or in the plaza. I wouldn't admit to myself that I was searching for her, only that I couldn't erase from my mind the way her full lips framed that hint of a smile, nor the way she carried herself with such easy confidence, nor the sensation of being intimately seen just by her glance, nor the memory of her scent, nor the way the wind passed through her pale blonde hair, nor the innocent sensuality she exuded without the slightest pretense. She was utterly different from me. These impressions of her were etched in my mind. I felt out of sorts. Worse still, I realized that I was steadily fabricating an intrigue, a fantasy that somehow found the two of us together, chatting, laughing, me somehow being near her, touching her, kissing her. These thoughts and feelings shocked me to my core, as if I scarcely recognized myself.

This village I call my winter home is unique for this region in that the local natives and expatriates who have taken up residence here have found ways to mutually benefit each other and yet still maintain the flavor of what was once a sleepy surfing town. Today, although Sayulita Mexico has been discovered, with many visitors arriving during season, it is a blended community that has kept its local identity centered around the plaza, church, and surfing beach.

Tonight, there would be a gala on the hillside overlooking the village. It was meant to benefit the water sanitation efforts of the town and it had been planned for some time. I'd been pressed to buy a ticket by the committee chair, a busy woman who brought her organizing talents to town once her own fundraising season was complete in Denver. She was, in fact, difficult to deflect and had extracted a promise from me to attend. There would be a BBQ dinner, dancing to a lively band, and an auction of local folk art, not to mention a generous tequila tasting table to encourage the gringo guests to feel magnanimous about parting with their money. As the day wore on I felt less and less enthusiasm until, resigned, I forced myself to dress and make what was intended to be a short appearance.

Entering through the large palapa, extravagantly decorated with twinkling lights, brightly colored flags, and streamers, I realized that arriving fashionably late may not have been the best plan. A long line had already formed for the BBQ, another at the tasting bar. Crowds of people stood about in clusters talking animatedly. Many of them I recognized but scarcely knew though they wintered here regularly as I did. I edged my way out to the far side where tables had been set along the bank overlooking the ocean. I stopped to chat with the delightful woman who keeps a shop across from the café. Then, from the corner of my eye, I saw her.

She stood alone on the edge of the bluff, gazing out to sea. I excused myself as quickly as politely possible and made my way toward her with increasingly nervous anticipation. I noticed immediately what was holding her fascination. A pod of blue whales was leaping and spouting as if performing for her alone. I was surprised to find that none of the revelers were paying the slightest attention to the magnificently choreographed water ballet as the creatures leisurely and playfully migrated north.

When no one else approached and I decided that she was indeed alone, I couldn't contain myself a second longer. I stepped close to her and in that moment it seemed completely natural for me to place my hand on her shoulder and introduce myself. She was neither startled nor did she pull away. She merely looked deeply into my eyes, riveting me to where I stood. With that same hint of a smile, she said, "How delightful to meet you. You dance, don't you, Diana?"

Startled, I felt suddenly transparent to her. How did she know my name? How could she know that I'd taken up ballroom dancing several years ago, shortly after my husband died? Hurriedly, effusively, I described to her the impact that she had had on me since first seeing her in the cafe. Words spilled from my mouth in an inane ramble of thoughts and impressions. I was horrified. I seemed to have lost control of myself.

"And do you write as well?" she asked, extending her hand in greeting. "My name is Savannah."

It was a relief to be interrupted.

"Well yes, I do write, a little. But what gave you that idea?"

She turned to fully face me and explained that she sensed by the way I had placed my hand on her—trustingly and yet with a felt intention—that I danced and probably well. She was kind enough not to comment on my embarrassing torrent of emotional verbiage and continued, "I'm a writer and so I resonate with the way you use language, the words themselves as well as how you just expressed yourself in a certain cadence, at once erupting and constrained. I've come to associate something subtle in the way you spoke with writers. Nonfiction though, correct?"

I was adrift, lost in her sea-green eyes, relishing her attention. I didn't want to admit that although I do write, my writing is of interest only to colleagues within my field of practice and possibly quite dull. "Yes, nonfiction," was all I could now mutter, aware that I was becoming vested in my need to appear interesting to her. Standing next to her evoked a surge of unprecedented feelings; all my attention was required just to remain calm.

I was taken further by surprise when I heard myself suggest that we stroll down to the beach so we could talk where it was quiet and—now I was also scandalized to think—more private. I wanted—I needed—to be alone with her. But what on earth did I mean by that? Smiling and receptive, she took my arm, waiting for me to move, or so I assumed. I was mortified to realize that just the slightest touch of her hand had rendered me too stunned to do so.

"Diana, I think there is a path just over here. It's probably the best escape."

Yes, escape was surely the word and her suggestion propelled me in the direction she had indicated. She apparently knew this village well. The path in question was neither well marked nor generally used. Who could this woman be? No one seemed to notice as we strolled away from the party and down the trail to the beach. The moonlight brilliantly reflected the phosphorus dancing atop the waves, slithering in gentle streaks when breaking along the shore. This evening was unfolding in an unprecedented and exhilarating manner. I felt something shifting within me yet had no concept of what that might be.

I had in mind some beach chairs away from the promenade. She seemed to read my mind and pointed toward two sun-faded blue loungers set a distance apart from the others. She clasped my hand, pulling me along in her wake. The sensation of her soft hand in mine made me dizzy, nearly breathless. She set about arranging the chairs immediately next to each other so that as we reclined I melted into the nearness of her. She sat next to me in silence as I, with butterflies fluttering inside my entire body, filled the salty air with chatter about the warmth of the soft breeze, the glint of the moon on a distant fishing boat, about how the way the whales' antics seemed to delight her. She continued to gaze out to sea, now and then turning to me with a disarming smile and what I can only describe as a glint of iridescence shining from her green eyes, identical in color to the sea's twilight hue and phosphorus shine.

In these brief moments outside-of-time, I told her some of my history. I tried to describe what had been most meaningful to me about my work, and as I was about to share my dreams, I realized that even as she appeared to listen intently, encouraging me by her intensity, it was I who was revealing all and she had scarcely spoken. Yet I felt as though we were engaged in the most intimate conversation. I couldn't say I had learned any more details about her than before but somehow I felt as though she had shared herself completely.

I was conflicted, scandalized to admit to myself that I desperately wanted to touch her, trace her jaw with my fingers, smell her hair. I wanted to experience her. That jolting thought had the immediate effect of an electric shock on my trembling body. Whatever did I mean by *experience her*? What was happening to me? I was terrified of offending or frightening her in any way and I prayed she didn't notice my obvious distress. As I struggled to gain control of myself, she said, "I don't scare easily, Diana, and I am enjoying experiencing you here in the moonlight as well. But I'm also quite thirsty and would like to find a bottle of water sometime soon."

I nearly choked, wondering if I had unconsciously spoken my thoughts out loud or if she could actually read my mind. If the latter were the case, she already knew that my mind was wandering all over her body. I had no idea what to make of her or of my own feelings. I had no idea how to behave. I only knew that I had to invent a way to get closer to her. I bravely suggested that my rooms were nearby where I could offer her iced bottled water. She seemed delighted by the prospect, which thrilled me. We were going to my rooms and we would be alone. The gala on the hill was all but forgotten.

But as we strolled down the beach in our bare feet, me carrying my socks and shoes clumsily against my chest and she twirling her sandals around her fingers from one hand to the other, I found myself nonplussed, uncertain how to proceed. I was worried that she could read my mind and I didn't want to think—let alone do—anything that would disrupt the strange familiarity I felt next to her. She was incredibly open and sensual. I had never felt this way, least of all for a woman, and I was confused and enmeshed in incomprehensible thoughts and feelings. And I couldn't control the sensations occurring in that certain part of my body that had been asleep for years. I craved the way I felt with her. I had no idea what to do or how I could approach her even though she was so genuinely receptive and forthcoming. I never expected nor could I have been prepared for what happened next.

My rooms were cool and refreshing and she commented that the breeze gently rustling the gauze curtains made them appear to be dancing in the moonlight. I purposely left the lights dimmed while I busied myself with waters and ice, found some salted nuts and a melon to slice. She wandered about, commenting on the few pieces of folk art I had managed to collect. She seemed especially drawn to a tiny painting of a mermaid I had only recently purchased from a local artist. I impetuously took it off the wall and gave it to her. Capturing me in her penetrating green eyes, she nodded and said, "I've always loved mermaids. Thank you, I'll treasure her."

Her hand lingered on mine as she accepted the glass of water. I felt dizzy and disoriented. She drank it all at once and nibbled on a piece of melon, watching me as I nervously plumped the pillows on the chairs and sofa. When she came close behind me, placing her hand on the small of my back, I froze solid. She turned me around to face her. Her eyes mesmerized me and my mind went blank. She clasped my hands in hers and led me to my bed. The maid had turned it down while I was out and we glided across the floor to a heaven of white cotton. I hardly recognized where I was. I scarcely recognized who I was. With a playful nudge, she invited me to lie down. Then curling her body next to mine, she wrapped her arms around me. She kissed me first on my cheek then several places on my neck before lingering on my lips, her tongue playfully licking and inserting itself, easing open my clamped mouth.

I went into shock. I was paralyzed, unable to move. I heard her giggle softly, whispering in my ear that she felt comfortable with me, that she tingled with pleasure lying next to me. I thought I heard her say that she would like to show me how she felt so that I could experience it as well. I heard her speaking. I could not respond.

She opened my blouse and slid her hand into my bra releasing my breast, her eyes locked on mine. I closed my eyes tight. She removed my shirt, then reached beneath me, unhooking and pulling loose the straps of my brassiere. I didn't stop her. I didn't want her to stop but I didn't know how to respond. Shivering in heat, my nipples hardened as she touched them and massaged them. She took one into her mouth and my vagina contracted in a spasm that I only vaguely remembered from some long ago time.

Gracefully she lifted herself over me and unzipped my slacks. Even with my eyes closed I could feel her intense focus on me. I felt myself enter a surreal landscape. I couldn't believe what was happening to me. My fantasy hadn't ventured anywhere near this with her. I was washed up on a foreign shore uncertain of the customs or the language. Still unable to move, unsure of myself, I was almost afraid—yes, afraid—of the shocking way I felt. She touched me gently, gliding her hands over my skin, which was now moist with perspiration but reacting as if I was chilled. Tugging my slacks down past my knees, she then pulled away my underpants. I flinched. Finally she yanked them both off my legs and threw them across the room.

I chanced to open my eyes just then and saw her gazing at my crotch. Her lips parted seductively as she looked directly into my eyes and said, "Diana, would you like to share a very memorable experience? I'd love to reveal you to yourself if you desire. I can open you to pleasures it appears you have not experienced for a long time or maybe you've never known before. Just say yes and I can make it happen for you." I gasped incoherently and closed my eyes again. "So it's yes. I sense how much you'll enjoy this exquisite experience, even if you don't know what to expect. Don't be afraid. You can trust that I know how to give you what you want and need."

She placed her hands softly on my heart and I felt a lovely ease come over my body. "Breathe, Diana, let yourself simply receive my care." She caressed my stomach and slid her hands softly down the inside of my thighs as my innermost being quaked with pleasure. How long had it been since my skin had been touched? How long since I had received a mere hug? She fondled my breasts and slowly explored my body with her gentle massage. As I warmed to her touch and began to relax I was aware of my face giving way to a smile. The way she had of tracing her fingers along my body felt miraculous. Simultaneously her fingers slid along the outside creases of my labia. I hadn't even touched myself there in years. Now her mouth, warm with her breath covered my opening. I nearly fainted. Her tongue licked me in that place, lingering, sucking my clitoris until I began to shake. My eyes opened involuntarily, coming into focus on the strap of her dress falling off her shoulder exposing her small round breast. She paused for a moment, smiling at me as she hiked her skirt up around her hips. I gasped and realized I hadn't been breathing. Then she lifted herself and kissed me on the lips, stretching over me, her fingers now touching me in that place between my thighs that was waking up, tingling as if having been compressed for eternity and now exalting that circulation had restored it to life. Savannah aroused me in ways I hadn't known existed for me, within me. I had to close my eyes again.

"Diana, I want to tell you about yourself. I want you to experience yourself in a new way. I want to give your mind some words to match what I know you are feeling in your body so that you can allow yourself to surrender to the pleasure locked within you. Later, not only will you remember these feelings, but in your mind, where you customarily live, you will associate my words in a visceral way. You can relive again and again the sensations you are discovering now." I may have nodded in assent. I could do no more. I was certainly hypnotized. Just as my consciousness stirred itself to the idea that she might actually be hypnotizing me, she continued, "Your breasts are full and just as sensitive as they were when you were young. Now when I suck on your nipples you'll feel electricity travel to your clitoris and the spasm you're feeling—feel it now Diana," she commanded, "you'll feel your entire body begin to throb as I continue. Allow this. We're just beginning on your journey of sensual sexual exploration. Relax. Soon you'll erupt in an orgasm like you've never known before. Maybe you have never before experienced a true mind altering full body orgasm at all, but you'll become intensely conscious of this gift. You will want it."

I hadn't known my fists were clenched nor my jaw. I opened my hands and touched her. Her short sundress had slipped off her shoulders. I touched her breast.

"Yes. I like that too. Touch me like that. Now feel this." She inserted her fingers into my vagina and my body bolted forward, my legs released and fell open wide. She stroked my clitoris and sucked my breast and I began to tremble. "Can you feel how wet you are? Luscious." Some unrecognizable part of me was shouting Yes! Yes I can! But I'm not certain any sound came from my voice. She caressed my breasts again and slid down my body, opening my legs wider, gently stroking the insides of my thighs, her fingers spreading my opening, massaging the edges of my ability to maintain composure. Her mouth, her tongue hot against my flesh, her fingers searching deeper, touching a place inside of me I hadn't known existed, a place that now pulsed on its own, sending its pulse throughout my entire being. I grasped her shoulders and my body released itself in a swirl of sensation, spasms, and moans. I tried to hold myself together. "There," she murmured. "Like that. Let it ride, Diana. Let your body writhe, let your voice cry out, let yourself be this miracle. For this pleasure you're allowing is surely a miracle and we're only just beginning."

Just beginning? I had never once been here before, never once felt like this before. Her words came to me from some far-off place, distracting me from my efforts to control myself. Was this the way I was meant to feel? In all my years of marriage I had enjoyed a certain warmth and pleasure with my husband and I was content. I hadn't known there could be more. I had no frame of reference. She eased her penetration and I collected myself as best I could. But now, suddenly she was pulling off her dress, slipping out of her panties, taking my hand and placing it between her legs. Showing me where to touch her.

Her nipples hardened and she cried out in ecstasy, her entire body vibrating intensely. She was incredibly beautiful in her moment of bliss and I struggled with a spasm of envy wondering how she was able to be so uninhibited and free with her sexual expression. I perceived that she had not so much learned but invited and allowed herself these pleasures. I was distracted from my own building desire when she arched her back and groaned from deep within herself, rocking rhythmically. I came apart from my restrictions and joined her, emboldened by her model, encouraged by her example.

We rocked, she on top of me straddling me still, my hands now pawing her, out of control, my mouth reaching blindly for her breast. I thrashed, unable to contain myself. She clutched one of my hands and pulled it down between her thighs again, guiding it back inside of her while she adjusted herself. I discovered what she wanted. I wanted to be able to give it to her. She taught me. And she let herself go again, even further than before. She was untamed, unabashed, and unashamed to give herself fully to her pleasure. Through her orgasm she held my incredulous stare, then suddenly she smiled and winked at me and we laughed. Or was I crying? Could that be possible? I felt a strange release of both sensations at once.

She made this happen so easily and she made it feel right. It's natural for her. She rolled off me and pulled me close to her, kissing my mouth voraciously. Then she burrowed her fingers into me again finding that place, taking me to a pinnacle over which I careened and then I was nothingness expanding deeply into a universe that was her. Inside my head I heard a crescendo like the choirs of heaven, or was she singing? Lost in sensations, in a profound sense of luxurious gratification, I was aware of her gracefully provocative undulations next to me, within me.

Now the distinct sensation of wanting to cry washed over me. I haven't wept in over five years, why now, in the midst of this ecstatic pleasure? Eventually, I discovered that she was indeed singing, singing to me softly, quieting herself, waiting for me to come to where she was. She sang me in from the void, calling me with tones I somehow recognized. Her essence hummed to me, welcoming me back to her touch, her scent, her kiss. I made a wish. I prayed that the pure joy of this moment would never end.

"It doesn't have to end," she whispered softly, that hint of smile concealing secrets only she possessed. She locked me into her mysterious eyes and kissed my lips tenderly before she pulled away from me just slightly and said, "Watch." And I watched as she took my hand in hers and spread open her legs, positioning herself so I could vividly see her moist pink tenderness. She guided my hand to her opening. "Watch," she commanded again. And I watched as she took my fingers and touched herself with them. I watched as she began to pulse. I watched as she began to shimmer. She willed me to discover her, go further with her. I leaned into her and felt my mouth seeking her, being pulled closer by her irresistible gravity. My lips touched her there, my tongue slid inside of her. I had no thoughts, no volition, only the most exotic visceral urge to please her, taste her, inhabit her world, dive into her essence. "Yes!" She shouted. "Oh, yes!" she moaned and shuddered into another wave of incredible pleasure that astonished me with its intensity and power. I saw her face illuminated in a bright sliver of moonlight, or was she emanating that brilliance? She moaned and writhed, her beautiful face— her beautiful smile—ethereal. "Watch," she demanded again. I was mesmerized, I could do nothing but. "Watch me and feel this. These are the orgasms you have wanted all your life. You can have this. You experienced this and you can feel this now again, through me." I could. I could feel in my own body each of her thrusting pulsations.

It was then I understood how much she frightens me. She frightens me with her power and freedom. She frightens me with her focused attention on my thoughts and yet I have never been so deeply and intimately affected by anyone in my entire life. She glided next to me like the rhythm of the tide, until she was spent, then whispered, "Please don't be afraid, Diana. You can have your heart's desire if only you know what it is."

Curling into my arms, eventually she drifted into sleep, but I lay still and awake for hours unable and unwilling to move, not wanting to disturb what must certainly be a dream. The moon sank in the sky outside the open doors of my balcony, casting a soft glow over her pale golden hair and smooth, tanned skin. I inhaled her intoxicating essence, drunk with the pleasure of her. I was lying with a woman. I was learning to make love with a woman. I had an orgasm. I've come alive because of a woman. I could never have imagined this wild possibility before.

My mind recalled each moment leading up to this one, acutely aware of the pressure of her body that was now peace-fully folded against mine. She's strange, a mystery. And I would gladly swear on a bible as truth the fact of a soft glow and nearly inaudible, imperceptible tone emanating from her. I listened to her gentle breathing in rhythmic harmony with the waves on the shore outside.

Though her, I was presented an opportunity to deeply feel the natural pleasures of lusty sexuality for the first time in my life. She caused me to feel known and appreciated, at ease and more fully attentive. Her focused presence in sharing her body wisdom with me in such intimate ways was a grace I couldn't have expected. Next to me lay an answered prayer I hadn't known nor had the faith to pray for.

As I turned to embrace her fully and hold her more closely to me, I was struck again by her warmth and beauty. Even as she slept, there was that faint hint of a smile on her inviting lips. I brushed her cheek with my fingers and discovered the trace of a tear had escaped her eye. I kissed her softly, the taste of salty sweetness on my lips. She stirred and pressed closer to me, tenderly laying her hand on my cheek.

Then I wept. Overwhelmed with emotion, long repressed tears spilled down my cheeks releasing me as if finally unshackled. I couldn't bear to think of awakening without her and I held onto her as if she might evaporate. It further distressed me to concede that she was a woman whose life was spent trusting her interests and intuitions. She didn't belong to me.

"That's true, Diana," she whispered, "there's no use in tearful lamentations. The blessing is that we met. The honor is that we shared an intimacy that can only be savored, never owned." I gasped. Again she had read my mind. She was an enigma but nothing about me was a secret to her.

"And now that you have tasted these pleasures that are possible for you, your mind will seek and gladly open to sample life's bountiful sweetness."

These sleepy words lingered in the moonlight and in my thoughts. And when I awoke at dawn she was gone. Nothing but a tiny pink shell and her mysterious scent lay on her pillow.

Once in winter I was granted pure bliss.

Though lovers be lost love shall not.
  ~ Dylan Thomas

Writing About Them for Me

When it comes to the feelings I possessed about him—that one who tripped me up, battered my ego, tempered my patience, proffered countless lessons in humility, and inadvertently nudged me toward becoming an author—what predominated was the gluttony of tantalizing desire. Am I the only woman of a certain age who absolutely should know better, but doesn't? I'm guessing probably not.

The folly of falling over the edge for an uninformed, un-evolved, un-involved man was apparently a lesson I'd yet to learn. I wasn't in the market for a project but sometimes I think the Universe, with its quirky sense of humor, enjoys pitting its constituents against ever more elaborate tests in order to refine or even redefine one's character.

Never mind that he was so much younger he couldn't help himself. His lack of relationship experience wasn't his fault. He hadn't lived long enough to experience most of those edifying landmines that men and women navigate together on the way to maturity. Never mind that he had no idea what he was doing with me nor I with him. That he let go of me every other week just sparked me to ramp up my "simply irresistible" quotient in response. This became a major work-out. And yet, the minute I became so fed up with the effort and said "Okay, fine," and let him go too, the phone rang and he came running back for more. Never mind that neither of us had a clue what more meant.

Why would a woman of some merit and accomplishment continue to lay out the welcome mat for chaos and frustration? A little dip into my writing history might provide some insight. But at the present moment, I'm writing about them for me.

I began journaling at a young age to make sense of my life experiences. In retrospect, a quick glance at the indulgent pages in the stack of notebooks and diaries I've accumulated clearly suggests that I was driven to scribble about moments of sadness and disappointment, frustration and confusion. When my day was filled with smiles and happiness, it rarely occurred to me to make time to reflect upon those pleasures. Maybe that was because happiness elicits a sense of carefree joy and lightheartedness, whereas sadness is like trying to find comfort on a slowly deflating air mattress that lands you on the cold ground. Add a depth of despair and ordinary sadness becomes like a nasty puncture wound with a barbed hook that if left untended, festers and torments. Angst and distress fueled my compulsion to write, first as a way to chronicle and unravel the true stories of my life and hopefully then to release the ache of emotional pain.

Meditation, soul searching, poetry, gratitude journals, prayer—have any of these time-honored tools of enlightenment advanced my introspection? Did any add to my emotional or spiritual proficiency? Has anything at all provided the necessary insight to match my maturity level to my actual age? I'd like to think so but it's such a lifelong process that on a daily basis I can't really tell. What about those of you who have followed these paths? Is there a shorter, easier route to contentment? I began to recognize that I've been writing the same story arc over and over, decade after decade. The locations and supporting characters change, but the essential nature of the curve remain. I often wonder if this pattern holds for other women and writers, in particular, or if it is uniquely my curve to bear.

One blustery winter evening at my home in the Pacific Northwest, I was lounging in a comfy loveseat, warm and cozy by the fire, enjoying a glass of wine with my computer on my lap. I was resolved to escape my self-indulgent journaling and begin writing the "important work" about love I'd imagined myself an expert on.

Caveat: I came to the assumption that I had anything important to write about love from the backside. I am not an expert on love. I am an expert on the facsimile of love, on the desire for love, on the disappointment of not having a love, on un-love. After many false starts, discouraging dead ends, and deleted pages I arrived at a blank space in my experience and worse—in my imagination. Clearly, the topic was magnificently beyond my grasp and I finally concluded I was ill-equipped to add one new valuable thought to the already vast library of writing, theater, poetry, paintings, and song already in existence.

My resolve went astray into a deep trench of exasperation that, for a change, wasn't focused on the fault of anyone else. That frustration was shackled to my own inexpert ability to communicate my complex thoughts on the subject and compose something meaningful. I do have one negligible skill: I can be tenacious in my ability to distract myself, so after hours of arduous unproductive effort, I reached for my dog-eared Tarot deck. Closing my eyes and setting an intention to gain insight into the matter, I plucked one card from the middle of the deck: the Eight of Swords. That's the one with the image of a blindfolded woman bound with rope, enclosed within a prison of tall swords. The meaning: constraint, disillusionment, frustration, obstacles, and restrictions. Fuck.

I backed up to consider my recent couple of relationships. The nature of each failed to provide any miraculous insight to the project. I had already begun to believe that the composite of characteristics and attributes I desired in a partner couldn't be found in just one man. This core belief convinced me that I could easily handle ongoing simultaneous affairs. Was I polyamorous? I once thought so, but more I believed the possibility of locating just one man with the combined best attributes would be a rare and precious find. I cobbled these traits together from the men I was involved with at any given time.

One's attraction was his high intellect. This was countered by his low emotional empathy. But we had great sex. Another's draw was his hunkalicious body and high energy. That's all he could offer. He required constant activity and meaningful conversation eluded him. But we had great sex.

There was the sweet SNAG (sensitive-new-age-man) whose inability to make a decision or resist pouting and emoting his way through a single day left me exhausted and mean-spirited. But we also had great sex. Then there was the party athlete. He sure did know how to have fun-fun-fun, but keeping up with his package was often a miserable morning-after headache. Still, we had great aerobic sex.

It occurred to me that if I focused my investigation on what was compelling about just one of them, besides sex, I might discover a treasure or sleuth out a morsel of meaning. The one I chose had common denominators with the others. He could be a stand in for any of them in that he offered me a series of vexations to write about. He is the one I frothed about in the opening paragraph as a model for the topic at hand. We shared a certain kind of love, but neither of us could get close to the ideal. What was it that made him more compelling? Without doubt we had that elusive thing: a seductive magnetic force that made us stick. And yes, I'll admit that we were mostly lust junkies. In those days, I suspected that the depth and true intimacy I longed for was a rare experience that existed for everyone else but me. Lust and aggravation would be our destiny together. I didn't know any better.

Lust is certainly not a mundane premise to explore, but in lieu of the lofty hypothesis I had all but given up, what could I do but default to journaling? The theme had all the elements required of story writing: a surprising beginning, a middle containing a series of obstacles, of angst, of fleeting authentic declarations, fabulous sex, wretched discontent, terrible sex, ridiculous hopefulness, endless questioning, more great sex, disillusionment to overcome, and finally a conclusion of sorts. I was merely spewing into my journal because, ultimately, what was the point? I didn't suppose that this story mattered to anyone but me and at that time I simply hoped to learn a core lesson once and for all. Unfortunately, even at this late date, revelations gleaned are still unconfirmed.

That man posed problems I struggled to solve both in the moment and existentially. By placing my attention on *him* as the epitome of *them*, I began to synthesize the essence of the old story. I searched for the bottom line, the underlying pattern, the gnawing unlabeled essence. As in the art of parfumerie, no matter how many other fragrant top notes I might ascribe to the story, lust was always the base note that held it all together.

Writing experts always suggest starting with what you know best. I know the startling swoosh of the rollercoaster ride through the dark mysterious tunnel of love. And thus, with a few bawdy ideas as my muse, I began to write the spicy stories that became this series of books.

Late one night, I arrived home from visiting friends in southern California. It was a miserable flight and I was still thinking about how much I had come to not only dread but detest air travel since terrorism put American airports in a chokehold. I was especially disgruntled since I was booked to travel across the country later in the week. That was the night I stayed up till dawn writing the story entitled "The Man in the Middle," which made its debut in *Waking Up*, Book #1 of this series, *Pleasure as a Higher Calling*.

I got a kick out of writing that short story and giggled when it was completed. Once I got a jumpstart on the idea, it wasn't a monumental struggle to craft a juicy short tale and then another. I put aside the idea that my very important work on Love would ever find a way out of me. Learning to enjoy writing rather than paralyzing myself with critical appraisal was the goal and ultimately I discovered that writing these spicy stories for the pure pleasure in it became my therapy as well as a creative vehicle for fun and laughter. Along the way, unpacking some of those scuffed-up bags of relational drudgery became my *raison d'être.*

Eventually I became published and my spicy stories surfaced on Amazon, available to all the world. Why would that be an issue? Isn't recognition of one's work the ideal of becoming an author? I hadn't thought ahead about how I would talk about the project to anyone but the editor, publisher, and a few friends. I rushed into the process in the same way I've jumped into relationships, adventures, ideas—off a cliff with open arms—ignoring the flapping of red flags in my wake only to realize mid-leap that I hadn't considered how or where to land.

Case in point: upon learning that I'd published a book of spicy romance stories, albeit fictional, one of my sisters was aghast to think of what our mom might have thought had she lived to realize her daughter had become a smut writer. Okay, that was fair and might have been expected since our mom would definitely have been scandalized. But when several acquaintances let me know they were shocked that I would jeopardize my reputation and social standing by writing about sex, I was frostbitten. Really? I thought most people, from the beginning of time, had an intrinsic interest in one of life's most sought after activities.

Then came the inquiries from a couple of male friends convinced a certain character was modeled after them. Dudes, it's fiction. But weren't the stories about my lovers? Sometimes yes, but mostly no. The less interesting truth is that the stories are based on composites of experience, character attributes of people I know, and yes, sometimes men I have loved or at least lusted after. But the details are imaginary. It's fiction. Can you believe that? No one seems to believe me, but it's what I always say. *Pleasure as a Higher Calling* is Fictional Memoir.

Back to Jonas, the guy I decided to focus on first. He unwittingly provided a treasure trove of lessons, passion, confusion, and problems to solve. I've written volumes of notes about how we met, why we shouldn't have met, and how we got hooked in energy. Pages more cover how I should have been more astute, could have staved off the tribulations or, had I been stronger, simply called it off. Instead I went with it because I had to since my most serious addiction is curiosity.

Jonas was a feast for my senses, strong and self-contained, but at the same time he could be commanded. He was taller than I am but not so tall as to crick my neck when we kissed. He had dark eyes and smooth skin and muscles that rippled in exertion. His lips were lush and he liked to kiss and he actually knew how. However, he gave only to receive. He was jealous and possessive but wouldn't fully connect or commit. He loved fellatio but couldn't bring himself to perform cunnilingus, so he wasn't fair, was he? He had drive and goals and misplaced values. He craved love and stability, but couldn't justify his feeling about me. That trait we shared. Are my assessments about him just, accurate, and fair? Yes. He was and is many things and as the years have passed, he's matured into a man I can admire, but that admiration had to be earned over time and would come many years forward. Our story inhabits the unhinged past.

It interested me that he couldn't exhaust me. His every ploy fueled me to become an excellent sales person hell-bent on overcoming his objections, issues, and problems. He said I was too intense. What does that mean? Too old to be so sexy. What's wrong with that? Too much. Too much what? He strived to find reasons to sabotage our connection, ruin our friendship, place wedges between us, cause chaos, practice his immaturity, get over on me. Did he succeed? Yes, but not completely. His resistance inspired me to maniacal persistence. Back then he was becoming aware of his power but he hadn't learned to use it well and effectively. And though I'm loath to admit this, I willingly gave my power over for the curious fun of experiencing him—as stimulating, sweet and wretched as it was at times. I also admit I used my power to manipulate him, for which I am not at all proud. In his case, I don't think my ceaseless curiosity and need to understand all I could about us, made me a masochist. I could be wrong. I wrote about him for me.

That time he played the gigolo? He said he was desperate and needed help. Could I loan him some money? I gave him some money and anyone can guess how that ended. Then there was the time he called, hell-bent on seeing me right away. He needed to talk to me; he couldn't wait to make love with me. Of course, I rearranged my plans, stayed in, and waited. He didn't show. He didn't explain. Who would put up with that shit? Me, back then. I wrote often about him for me.

What about that time I sprained my ankle severely and was in agony? He picked me up from the hospital, helped into the house and onto the couch, then sat across from me silently watching me. "What are you doing?" I asked. "I'm waiting," he mumbled. "For what?" I asked. "You. I'm ready now; let's go in the bedroom. It'll only take fifteen minutes!" Motherfucker.

And there was that one time, returning after a long day on the road. We had a couple of cocktails, started to make love, got to the thick of it when he passed out cold on top of me mid-orgasm. Who does that? What makes him the embodiment of both a wonderful experience and a ridiculous misadventure? I'm a writer. He was the main character in my life at that time. He was the jumpstart. I began to write about them for me because of him.

What about someone else? Someone with a different dynamic? I've thought about this. I can't truly blame every man I've been involved with for the angst and hilarity, the disappointments and ecstasy that resulted in our eventual demise, can I? Of course not. Let me choose another here to explain why writing about them for me is a homeopathic remedy.

Timothy. Tim. He preferred to be called Timoth, and was one of the most compelling men I'd been involved with, in that he remained a mystery to me for the longest time. Beguiling, solid, engaging, smart, funny, secretive, sexual. He seemed almost perfect. I figured he'd reveal more of himself eventually. In the meantime he remained aware of his good looks in a rustic, swarthy manly way: dark hair, freckled fair complexion and green, green eyes. Black Irish to the hilt. He had a certain musk to him that rustled up my libido. The slightest provocation from me would launch him on a mission to prove himself more passionately adept than the time before.

This is a great quality in a lover, right? Yes. Still, he was a stinker. Not a bad man, none of my lovers have been bad men. Just stinkers when it came to measuring up to certain criteria. My criteria:

1) He holds his own in a conversation because he can and wants to, not because he thinks he must to get laid.

2) He has a sense of humor about himself and life that provides him with enough tools to ward off endlessly defending his ego.

3) He takes care of himself and his business and isn't looking for a mother, mentor, or purse.

4) He is solid and confident and is likewise accepting that I am, rather than devising ways to undermine, repress, and control me or otherwise make my life miserable.

5) He thinks I'm sensational, interesting, sexy, and brilliant!

Is that asking too much? I offer up the above list as the first five minimal attributes I'm longing for.

Timoth's secret was difficult to uncover for an amateur empath such as myself. But once I discovered his underlying issue, it helped explain and perhaps even justify his maladaptive behavior not only toward me but the situations in his life. Let's run back over those criteria to better understand how we came to a disappointing demise. To be sure, his behavior could have been characterized as typical of the men attracted to me. Why I'm attracted to them is still revealing itself out in my own deep ruminations. The discovery that this man was like the last man in many ways and likely similar to the next, gave me plenty to write about.

It took a full year to convince me that Timoth failed the criteria:

1) True, he had a lively and entertaining repertoire of stories and experiences to keep me bemused, but an in-depth conversation about anything controversial or, God forbid, personal was off the table.

2) He could laugh, and he could appreciate my sense of humor. He was also excellent at demeaning any person or situation—and often me—in a joking way. "Just kidding! What's wrong, can't you take a little joke?" You catch my drift.

3) He could be a bit obsessive/compulsive about grooming, especially concerning his hair. His eating and exercise were planned for optimal input/output. He appreciated my real food healthy cooking while being picky as hell about every item in the finished product. Disclaimer: Rarely do I faithfully follow recipes. I can be eclectic in my choices of herbs/spices/flavors so can't always detail the exact ingredients I've tossed in the sauce or salads I create. At times I felt I like I was on the witness stand instead of at the dinner table, being interrogated by a food detective or a kid suspicious of anything that didn't look like mac and cheese.

4) His self-confidence revealed itself to be a facade, an experience I've discovered in my lovers time and again. Why? I am still asking myself this. He used his charisma to defend his position even when I wasn't in opposition. In the end, although he wasn't looking for a mentor or a purse, he really needed a mommy. Because I would encourage him, he sometimes acted on his emotions and let himself truly feel, even cry, but then berate me for making him feel bad rather than allow me to comfort him.

5) Mostly, I wanted a man to appreciate my best qualities, which I believe to be intelligence, emotional maturity, and strength. He liked that I was sexy. The rest was meaningless to him.

Why an entire year to discover the issue that explained his particular array of behaviors? I mentioned his penchant for secrecy. One lovely afternoon, a day without incident or conflict, we were sitting on a park bench overlooking the bay, talking about the lack of religious indoctrination in my childhood, which did not breach criterion #1 because it was about me, not him. He began to squirm and fidget, standing, sitting, pacing etc. When he eventually revealed his own angry history as an Irish Catholic altar boy, the shamed favorite of his parish priest, I was sympathetic. He began to resent me for learning his dark pain. Still we hung on.

In the course of a year, never once did he want me to suck his cock. Never once has a man refused me that delight. He also never once opened his eyes and looked at me while having sex, which I will give him was a tender, loving experience and never rough or aggressive. He was simply never able to be fully present to me in the most intimate of our times. We began to drift. I stopped making my usual over-the-top effort to make it all be something it couldn't. He simply lost interest and went home. I'm writing about him now for me.

Once upon a time I met Bill. I was experimenting with online dating, testing myself to discover if I could take it seriously. After the requisite digital back-and-forth and a couple of phone calls, he asked me out. He was an online dating professional and I was new to the game. From Bill, I got a crash course on why online dating can be so deceptive, time-consuming, disappointing, and exhausting. At first I thought we were on the same page. Neither of us could see the value in a protracted period of remote "getting to know you." I'd already discovered that meeting in person early on helped sidestep an accumulation of misrepresentation, bullshit, and outright lies, not to mention the deceptive pictures people post of themselves. So when he wanted to meet right away I agreed.

He was fairly attractive, a decent likeness of his posted pictures and refreshingly honest, which I found to be his best asset.

Over a single Starbucks, I leaned that he was attracted to me mostly for my looks and had only skimmed over my profile. Also, that he was only interested in sex and if I wasn't, he'd move on, since women who were swarmed the internet and many were already interested in him. I couldn't stifle my laughter when I realized he was serious. I told him I was only interested in fabulous sex and if he couldn't muster, I'd move on since I had more offers in my dating inbox then I had time for in this life. He wasn't amused.

He told me he didn't have time for women with issues. I told him I didn't have time for jerks although he probably knew plenty about jerking off thinking about the dozens of women already interested in him. I was joking but his red face and clenched coffee cup suggested to me that we were off to a challenging start.

He then professed his suspicion that I was a "wicked ball-busting bitch but likely a good fuck" so he might overlook my character flaws. His serious expression couldn't disguise the twinkling humor in his bright blue eyes, which faded as I described how his busted balls would shrivel and rust before I would consider overlooking his aberrant character. We laughed. We said goodbye. He didn't stop calling me for weeks, but I knew that not only did he not qualify, criteria-wise, neither did we have the chemistry, that thing, to sustain the storyline any further.

Now I'll share a little story about the chef who wooed me with delicious meals, divine sauces, and amazing confections. This talented man knew everything about cooking and pairing his delectable creations with the best wines. He made his own bread and cheese. But he could only cook in his own kitchen. He never once came to dinner at my place and would rarely let me help or make suggestions.

His name was Lessing, Less for short, because as he liked to joke, "Once you've had a taste of Less, more would be gluttony." A large, burly man with full, soft lips and sensitive, sultry eyes, he clearly enjoyed his own cuisine. He was eager to please me, fulfilled criterion #5 and we had fun together for a while.

He'd begin his seduction early in the day, emailing me the evening's menu, described in luscious detail, and he loved it when I'd bring just the right flowers or create a playlist of perfect music pairings for our many hours at the dining table. Our foreplay was fabulous food which compensated for his lack of stamina in bed. This is not to say that our sex wasn't stimulating or enjoyable, merely that he'd exhaust himself in the kitchen and was often drunk by the time we stumbled into bed. I have a lusty appetite and admit I preferred extra helpings of sex. Once he'd spent himself sexually and we'd already consumed the dessert of chocolate or cognac he'd garnish the evening by eating me until I was also sated and we'd spoon until breakfast. He couldn't bear to think I might be disappointed in any way and he learned to gently "knead my dough" and "slurp my oyster" and "sip my nectar" and generally "butter me up." These were all his corndog terms.

Food and cooking were his first passion and I began to get used to his culinary discourse during our lovemaking. We spent nearly all one winter together mostly at his place, our conversations and activity centered around shopping, prepping, blanching, baking, roasting, and sautéing, dining, sipping, and finally boinking. I began to desire a more elaborate menu of activity. A movie out instead of in. Live music instead of my playlists. A slow walk in the forest. A brisk walk along the waterfront. Dinner in a new restaurant.

These were often a hard sell for the chef, especially restaurants. He was like a skilled musician friend of mine who was compelled to critique and could scarcely enjoy another band's live performance. Once in a while, when I was able to convince Less to try a new cafe or bistro, he would find something on a menu he wasn't familiar with and dissect it flavor by flavor to discern how he could replicate it at home. Mostly he found cause to complain about the food in those rare instances we dined out.

Eventually, Less and I became less than more until one final morning before breakfast, I took my leave. I packed up my copper saucepan, toothbrush, extra five pounds, and headed home for a simple green smoothie and a long run.

Then there was the "take it easy," slow-talking, slow-walking Bernie. We met accidentally while walking in the park. I passed him more than once on that route in the course of several weeks. He walked slowly and since I was out to power walk, sometimes I passed him twice. One day we both stopped at the same bench to re-tie our shoes. After a friendly exchange of drivel, I powered on. The next day he was sitting on that bench as I came by. He greeted me with a wide smile, a warm handshake, and a coconut water. He was there every day from then on. He sped up and I slowed down and we walked together often from that point on. We also went for coffee. We went for pho. We went to the beach. We went for drinks. We went on errands.

Bernie may have had a slow, southern way of interacting with the world but he wasn't the least slow-witted. We could laugh ourselves silly over the slightest provocation. Eventually we went to my house and slowly slid into bed.

So what was it about Bernie that made my heart go pitta-pat? That man was solid. He was smooth and he made it his mission to please me. Also, that man was in possession of a skilled slow hand and slow voluptuous way of making love to me. At that time, he was exactly what I needed: no commitment required of me, all on my terms, at my beck and call and apparently happy to be counted among my lovers without balking at the knowledge there might be others. He also had an antebellum way of viewing the world and me. If I wasn't ladylike, he'd be visibly uncomfortable—except in bed. If I cussed, he'd mutter, "Oh my . . ." If I veered too far off the path of respectable Baptist behavior in conversation he felt compelled to remind me of the way back. I'm not a Baptist so this became a regular ordeal. When I finally begged him to shut the fuck up about religion, his religion, over dinner at my home one night, he put down his fork and began a one-sided soliloquy on why then-President Obama was not a Christian and possibly the rumors were true that he was Muslim. Rather than stab him, I put down my fork and asked him to leave.

One week later, he was at the park bench with a coconut water. That afternoon he asked me to lunch in a special spot he knew in the next town. We ordered a lovely lunch after which the check lay on the table between us for quite some time. It was time to leave and though he had invited me to go out, he was waiting for me to pick the tab. He said he'd left his wallet at home. I paid, then dropped him off without inviting him in. A week later he was sitting on the park bench with a coconut water.

I wasn't seeing anyone regularly at this time, so after a couple of weeks I let him come back home with me. To get back in my good graces he made love to me the way I like it: slowly with lots of oral attention and many satisfying orgasms. Later when I made no move to make dinner, he suggested we walk over to a bistro near my place where he replayed the forgotten wallet scenario again. I picked it up and we walked back, him real slow, me real fast. I let myself in and locked the door.

Going Dutch is not a big deal when that arrangement is mutually acknowledged, so was this really an issue? In Bernie's case? Yes. He never once followed through with making plans, picking up the check, having me to his place, or introducing me to friends even after he knew it mattered. I picked up the check one final time before the last goodbye. I would miss the easy sex focused on my pleasure, but I wouldn't miss him.

Although I could easily conjure up many more stories about the men I've enjoyed (or not) I'll finish with one last story for now. Randal was my age, which was a novelty at the time. He was tall, handsome, and retired. He had become a playwright, a romantic poet, and senile. We met online but lived at least a 90-minute drive apart so we conducted a rather long email and phone discourse. Once I likened him to Peter Pan stranded in Neverland. He resonated with the idea of never growing up and lamented to me how everyone he knew these days was old! Randal was convinced he was Mensa-level brilliant and he decided that I was a latent Mensa candidate and he would sponsor me.

I'd never met an actual live Mensa intellect. As it turned out he was not only forgetful but a bit delusional when it came to self-assessment. He wasn't a member of Mensa; he just thought he should be and suggested that if I hung with him long enough I would be too. One might wonder why I would take the time to get to know this man whose photos featured twinkling blue eyes on a lined face grinning happily at the camera. His blond grey hair peeked out from a Yankees baseball cap and in his hand was a book of poetry by Mary Oliver. He was unusual.

And he was whimsical, claiming he wrote well in beautiful cities like Montreal, Florence, and New York. He was certain that anyone could become a better writer if inspired by a beautiful place. He invited me to join him in Paris for a month so we could work on our projects in the City of Lights. A lovely offer, although we hadn't even met in person, so I broke the stalemate and told him I'd drive north on a cool sunny autumn Saturday.

He greeted me at the door with a mop in one hand and a broom in the other. When I arrived, he was still cleaning his small rented house on a quiet street lined with maple trees. He'd become immersed in baseball stats and forgotten I was coming. He thought he'd made a reservation at his favorite restaurant overlooking the sea, but called again just be sure. When we arrived he had two tables reserved, one in his first name and one in his last. I have to admit, after months of distal communication, I enjoyed his childlike enthusiasm for living in the moment and his company was easy and affectionate like we were old friends or even relatives.

We got a little drunk on Scotch over a lovely dinner and even though we were a bit wobbly, we took a long walk along the waterfront before stopping for a coffee so I'd be in better shape to drive home. Instead he invited me to stay over. I realized that driving wouldn't be wise and I also felt fine about accepting his invitation.

Randal was never called Randy. He confided that even when someone addressed him by his full name, all he heard was Ran, which he preferred. We made some tea and as I looked around I noticed what I hadn't before. He had only one bedroom and two overstuffed easy chairs in the living room. No couch. Sleeping with him was something I hadn't considered as yet.

Eventually, though, I did. Here's why: Ran was so sweet and innocent. He held my hand and asked me if I would kiss him since he was out of practice. I laughingly complied. His lips were soft and receptive and his eyes twinkled with delight. It was so endearing. Here was a man who had fathered three children, run a business, and written plays that were performed and applauded in his small town and yet his behavior was so guileless and un-calculated. He gave me a large Mariners T-shirt to sleep in and we climbed into his squeaky-springed double bed.

We faced each other talking for a long time. This wasn't the usual getting-to-know-you kind of sharing. His interests were in what I thought about sports in general, baseball in particu-lar, how a certain song made me feel and why, what my greatest thrill had been, my deepest sorrow. I wanted to know where he stood on the environment, how he felt watching one of his plays performed, his experience of becoming aware of memory loss. Deeper stuff.

Ultimately, we hugged and kissed and it became clear to me that he hadn't forgotten how to make love. What he had forgot-ten, because it had been so long, was the experience of orgasm. He set about pleasing me in delectable, sensual, caressing, oral, and penetrating ways for quite some time. He couldn't come. He didn't seem disappointed rather he was lighthearted about the fact of the two of us "Mensas" naked together in his bed. I decided to make an all-out attempt at getting and keeping him aroused, stimulated and hard to pleasure him. He was stiff and giggling when eventually I mounted him. I surprised myself with a voluptuous orgasm and in the same moment he ejaculated, squealing with delight. When I dismounted and rolled to the side in luscious tingles, he jumped out of bed and danced around the room laughing and shouting. All I could do was watch him in smiling wonder. After his bit of a romp, he sat naked at his tiny desk and composed a poem for the occasion. We didn't last. He was sweet. He had dementia.

So because each man I've dated met at least some of my criteria, eventually I came to understand and accept that in lieu of finding the one perfect partner, which was not happening for me, I'd juggle my time and energy among three lovers to compensate. A combination of their respective best traits made for an overall more fulfilling experience.

Over the course of time, one would be replaced with another of his ilk to keep the balance of three. True, there have been instances when I was simply a slut and glutton and slipped an extra lover into the mix, but that would become wearing to me in short order. Three lovely men, not all at once and not all the time, made for a sexually satisfying lifestyle. What it couldn't do was satisfy any yearnings for a deeper, more emotionally intimate relationship. It was what it was. It still is what it is. I compensate by calling my acceptance of this conundrum an admirable adaptation to my current realities and circumstances. I made the best of it and enjoyed the many benefits of attention, intense focus, and best of all, freedom.

Over the years the line-up would include the intelligent one, the creative one, the independent one, the musical one, the young one, the older one, the troubled one, the sensitive one, the funny one, the athletic one, and the married one. The common denominator for all was that each was unavailable in his own way for the Big Love, the love story I've yet to write. And so was I.

My friends wonder how I keep my sense of optimism and general *joie de vivre* in lieu of the gaggle of men I've loved. It's not complicated. I chose Pleasure as a Higher Calling and never looked back. I make the effort to find it in every aspect of my life.

I make an effort to share it with those who wish to receive. I still long for the man who won't come undone by my ability to establish for myself all the pleasure life can offer within my certain set of circumstances. One day he'll come along. I'm not absolutely sure of that. But if and when that magic time arrives, it will signal that we both have found The One in each other and are ready to explore the mysterious unfathomable realm of True Love. A lofty dream for sure.

For most of us, disappointment, misunderstanding, sadness, and loss can't be avoided. I have taught myself to find a degree of pleasure in fully feeling and expressing even those emotions that rip at my heart or sear my soul. I want to fully understand them in myself and others. To the extent that it is possible for me, I seek pleasure. Activities and people, babies, dogs and kittens, beauty, concepts and feelings that elicit pleasurable responses are easy to appreciate, aren't they?

These days I have gained that awareness and also take the time to notice and truly treasure those gifts. When it's a tough go or nearly impossible to find a way out of sinking into despair, but then I do, I relish in the pleasure of the courage I was able to garner to rise back up and smile again. Releasing the old mindset of "misery loves company," my company was a first step in discovering that pleasure could fill that void.

And I continue to write. It's about them but it's for me. And if my experience or thoughts on the matter helps at all, then I write about them for you too.

About The Author

Savannah Aries is a sassy, passionate, contemporary woman who claims and advocates *Pleasure as a Higher Calling*. Her spicy stories of life, love, sensuality and lust highlight the adventures of a juicy mature woman, creating, navigating and enjoying the new rules of engagement.

Women (and men!) of all ages are delighting in her humorous perspective, peppered with a bit of well-deserved angst, as she attempts to unravel and make sense of life's most enduring mystery: the luscious story of Love.

Savannah lives in the beautiful Pacific Northwest.

If you enjoyed *No Regrets*, you'll want to read the other books in the *Pleasure as a Higher Calling* series:

Waking Up

Easy & Delicious

Visit Savannah's Author Website:
www.savannaharies.com

amazon.com/author/www.savannaharies.com

Follow Savannah on social media:

facebook.com/savannah.aries

twitter.com/savannaharies

instagram.com/savannaharies6127

www.ingramcontent.com/pod-product-compliance
Lightning Source LLC
Chambersburg PA
CBHW032156190626
46808CB00021B/1366